Acid Taste:

Excavating the Homesick's Blues

ACID TASTE:

EXCAVATING THE HOMESICK'S BLUES

Émilie Galindo

Querencia Press - Chicago, IL

QUERENCIA PRESS

© Copyright 2024
Émilie Galindo

ISBN 978 1 959118 84 8

www.querenciapress.com

First Published in 2024

Querencia Press, LLC
Chicago IL

Printed & Bound in the United States of America

CONTENTS

FOREWORD

This book is a pandemic baby of sorts. I was subbing at the time, working on lessons focused on the Utopia as a literary trope. Reading very closely Charlotte Gilman Perkins' *Herland*. This then coalesced with the need for escapism and the questions raised by the existential crisis that hit us all.

I set out to write this book as a thought experiment. At first I was merely aiming to explore the limits of any possible utopian society. However, my fascination for the history and culture of the 60s has thankfully led me away from an explicit, but likely dry social commentary and toward something with the substance of nuance as well as subtext. Even though this book uses lingo, historical figures and cultural references rooted in the 60s; the decade doesn't limit the story. In fact, it is the wind of experimentation and idealism that we breathe while we explore the meaning and viability of utopias not only in the linear chronology of History, but in the cyclical pattern of human lives. Like Johnny Cash's song, the story asks: *what is truth?* And suggests that it's something understated, even subterranean.At the time I was then making my way through Toni Morrison's bibliography and had fallen head over heels in love with her use of magical realism to bring subtext to the forefront. Combined with surrealism, it was my into the characters' inner lives. A way of saying: we all come with our system of bias-carrying symbols.

This utopia is purposely not tied to one particular geographical location. The American historical references are hopefully offset by an architecture of life shaped by my upbringing in a multicultural neighbourhood in the south west of France. My hope is that this lack of geographical specificity will allow the story to steer clear of the El Dorado trope to focus on the people and their intentions. To drive home the message that an ideal is a construct not a place, therefore we have the power to build it.

Yes, it is a wildly experimental and crowded world. A pot of not so melted together characters spiced with all the creative minds who give me faith. I just want to pay it forward.

Something Like a Throwback or a Look Back: Pulpy Ride & Rocked Out Oranges & Can You Dig It?

Zzzeeeemmm goes the omnipotent & omniscient rotary phone as its dial spins counter clockwise.

Hello there, did you find it alright? It's pretty far from everything. I hope the ride wasn't too long, greets a woman wearing a navy blue skirt suit.

No worries. The landscape made for a pleasant ride.

Estela, right?

Just Ela's fine, is Ela's response as she briefly stops fiddling with her necklace to shake the other woman's hand.

Bonnie, she replies, bringing the palm of her right hand to the little patch of pink cotton on her chest. So, I don't mean to discourage you or anything, but are you sure about this?

Dead sure, yes.

Alright then. I really wasn't trying to discourage you by the way. I'd be shooting myself in the foot if I did. But, as you know, we tried and—

I know, I know. But it's different. We're already a community.

Something coats Bonnie's blank gaze.

Alright, she shakes the gaze & the coating away, let's see if the shoe fits, shall we?

A lemon-licked bus passes a clock tower,

its driver; a woman, Gloria, emerald-eyed & twinkling laugh,

zigs a glance at her watch,

it has stopped.

The bus pulls up,

over a particularly ambivalent looking patch of field bindweed & white clover.

The tail lights glow like incandescent wax.

Acapella snatches of The Who's *Magic Bus* float,

riding the Lila aroma highway of a past zeitgeist.

A colourful ragtag team of individuals file out of the bus, suitcases or bags in hand.

They're quipping, bantering, cracking jokes, all boisterously, and they make the bush

of Morning Glory sway as they enter the house.

You'll see, they're terrifically prolific trees.

Pretty too.

That they are. They really are. And a lot of work. Worth the—what—ten

wheelbarrows of rocks we unearthed to plant them.

How many were you?

At first six. Unfortunately it got all *Rumour*ed up and two split. The four of us who

stayed behind fought over what to do with this place.

That's too bad.

Yeah. I guess we thought we had it made. Man were we wrong.

The façade is pale, but the sanguine beams & shutters add the blood of good health.

15 adults & one infant penetrate the house.

Door wide open. Its curled brass hand left untouched. But maybe not unmoved.

Fingertips resting against the wood.

The first room is

a spacious yet modest Mediterranean style living-room

a staggered row of copper pots like exclamation marks on a sugar-white wall, solid

wood, wicker elephant side table, newspaper rack, cream sofa clad with a patchwork

afghan, delicate crochet flowers run looks like lily pads floating on the coffee table.

Lime snowflakes cool the sweetly simmering potpourris in voluptuous terracotta pots,

on both sides of the sofa.

Friendly, reliable, even a little dashing.

How many are you?

15.

Oh woww… I don't know…

That's including 5 couples, Ela specifies.

Haaa. Alright. There should be enough rooms then.

Oh yeah. Yeah, I thought it through.

Yeah, we planned to be a tribe too. We even flipped the garage as a wing early on.

Thinking more people would join us.

The woman in navy looks around. Rosemary stings her eyes.

Maybe it wasn't the place for us.

The other woman fiddles with her pendant—a brass compass with a pansy where the

Wind Rose should be.

The group scatters, interacts & comments.

A woman, Yasmina—gold concentric circles on her neck & ears & a leather-rugged

look—acknowledges the outer circle shaping the present sphere.

Another woman, Aimée—apple-cheeked & wing-eyed— caresses the turquoise &

white damask curtains adorning the bay window. By her side, a man is rocking an

infant in a Pacman reminiscent outfit.

A man, Az—a zellij on the tender skin of his right wrist & wah-wah charisma—

jokingly points out, "no foosball table? With this space? What a waste!"

A man, Sid—wearing a tartan flannel shirt & jeans & a folksy air & a signet ring that

reads SH—leads the others to the kitchen via the door on the left of the living-room.

Vertical rows of miniature lemon trees on the walls, a yellow formica table in the

centre of the room, with yellow, orange, & white kitchen cabinets framing the sink.

Good luck then, the woman says, straightening her skirt suit. With a silent but

perusing gaze she says goodbye to more than a house or a home.

You know you're always welcome to join us, Ella offers sincerely. Stroking the

compass with her thumb.

That's awfully generous of you. But no. It's haunted for me here, now. We dug it but

we didn't really *dig* it. I don't know if that makes any sense.

I totally *dig* you.

A woman, Luciana—harlequin maxi dress & feathers in her shaggy hair— opens the
yellow drapes
"Exudes some much felicity."
The woman with the pansy compass smiles. *Feliz.*
They count 4 rooms & 3 toilets & 2 bathrooms left of the living-room
Rooms, warm primary colours. Bathroom, cold primary colours.
They retrace their steps to visit the wing to the right of the living-room,
groovier tones, materials, & shapes
Harvest gold that hums *California Dreamin*, tambourine macramé, giggling bean bag
chairs, brick-chucking avocado green, drop out lava lamps, Allen Ginsberg coined
sofas, finally-freed-bird fringes, the Peace loving orange & red & brown.
Still buoyant, only *slightly* more mature.
3 dens or cosy rooms in the making & 1 bathroom/toilet.
1 den breaks away from the mould:
Blue wallpaper with colourful geometric shapes & a pinball machine & a TV with a
VCR. Flanked by two bookshelves of JVC VHS.
On the left side of the TV, in the corner, a bulky hifi system with a tower of CDs.
All the volume of the 80s.
Nouméa—deep black eyes but sweet & cloudless & quartz elegance—turns to Ela to
congratulate her,
"Heavens! Great job, Ela. You've really found a gem here."

Some have already flocked outside to the fenceless, gateless garden.
Abe, Sal, César, Jo, Lila, Yann & Za.
They bask in the day's distilled ale warmth
seemingly unable to peel their eyes away from the green and oranges ahead of them.
Mimosa hovers & drifts
like pixie dust.

Book I:
Do the Hustle

Nondescript Day

Click zem click zem click zem click zem click zem click zem goes the omnipotent & omniscient rotary phone as it's dialed clockwise

Drops of orange juice fall into the night.
An alarm shrieks, pouring shrill water in chamomile sleep. Morning's ***dot dot dot*** has already landed on the wall, and is suspensefully waiting.
On a wall, a bare peg pouts. On a coffee table, a gaunt bottle looks parched.
Everywhere, sprawling books yawn.
On a bedside table, a yelling and wiggling phone flashes doggedly.

Time!   It's   time   to   wake   up!

The dutiful and diligent device rings relentlessly, until a hand emerges from the bed and quiets the digital rooster with a pat.
Today's forecast sits—not so carefully folded—on a chair at the foot of bed.
A hand flops back onto the bed for a minute. We follow the path of the hand through a bed-marked arm to a woman.
By the bedroom door, a wonky rack carries seasons of flowers.
A woman extricates herself from the nook of night and trudges to the bathroom.
On the south wall of the corridor, a cotton-tailed friend frolics in a day-glo cloud of kaleidoscopic consciousness.

Mustard light spurts down from the ceiling. The hamper is boiling over. Restless
sleep has bruised her eyes. Water plays percussive porcelain.
Not that she notices.
It's one of those mornings.
Tugged strings mornings.
When **will** surrenders to **have to**.
Tugged by the purse strings.
Those mechanical mornings.
Buffering mind & programmed actions

Slathers | A smattering of consciousness
      Chest | 2 teaspoons of dreams
            Neck | bubbling outline of day
            Arms & Legs | skimmed motivation
            Nooks & crannies | smoky throwbacks & straitlaced lists
                Rinses | it doesn't, all swirls down the sink
Voluble worries whir & Looming light & Fidgeting, faltering and fumbling
On her bedroom door, a calendar looks pale and skinny. Jagged paper dangles as the
only reminder of the months before May. Xed days are gone. Windows of life barred,
like stubbing out a cigarette.
A sluggish chant billows from the remaining days' open windows

Carpe Diem
Carpe Diem
Carpe Diem
Sing
Children sing
Death is a-comin' in.

She unclenches shutters to let the eager light in. Yellow specks on the linoleum floor appear and soon coalesce in a jasmine tea tide that surges and colours everything it brushes.

Frozen handprints on the windowpane are left reaching in, or out.

18

Out she heads to the bus stop. Absent-mindedly walking the path carved into reality by repetition. Stiff strides.

Legs stretching like a clothespin. Soundbites of reality and fantasy as thoughts.

Waiting at the bus stop, she notices a worm slowly slithering toward her. Gashed asphalt bleeds weeds. Shaggy life poking through the prophylactic.

She makes a mental note to avoid stepping on the little guy when she hops on the bus.

Practical Pranking

The sunrise dries the night's lull while money acts as the yeast that makes the day rise. Or the jolt of electricity that brings stiff bodies down the conveyor belt. Playful beams caress curcumin & piment streaks on an acid lemon bus. A clumpy thatch tilts forward. A mischievously green grin punctuates the greeting. Doors clap. The bus resumes its itinerary. Briefly converging eyes scatter.

Headlines & storylines & memories & musings tacitly prevail over the sanctioned silence.
She is sitting in the front of the bus. Looking out the window, looking up to the grapefruit sun (which hasn't altered the pH of the sky). The radio's lime words muffle the impatient fizzling of the bus.

Out and in
>A grey & wheezing avenue / work cups the mind>
>A sad series of aphonic neons / headset & service & screen & customer>
>Apple cider motivation has turned into vinegar / bodiless voices beating the eardrums>
> Lemonade light calls for a barbecue / acrylic tapping grates>
Soon the in trumps the out
>Calls for glossy adventures to tack on the mind / arid reprieves>
>Duty free perfume & Toblerone trips >

She doesn't pay any attention to the mishmash of individuals riding with her.

>A Stone cold California blonde is sitting by the window in her knee-length tie-dye dress. She is in her late twenties. She is an elementary school teacher. She is late. Her thumbs are dancing frantically.

>A Groggy 50-something dude looks like the response to the question 'What if Father Time & ZZ Top had a child?' He sells fishing equipment. But he mostly reads, because not many people come by his shop anymore. People trust franchises more than passionate individuals.

>A couple of prim ladies leer at the California blonde & the groggy 50-something dude. They're fit and spry, cause 70 is the new 60. Clad in their floweriest pencil skirts. Their shopping trolleys resting on their knees.

>A group of teens are doing some last minute cramming before their big exam. Skinny jeans & *we're screwed* & bell-bottoms & *stop hogging the notes* & olive pedal pushers & *no time for a smoke* & ripped jeans & *fuck this I'm winging it* & they're all pretending they didn't study for this last night.

>A school of suits crowds the back of the bus. A whole lot of bowed heads, consuming the world through a consumed apple. Apps close to reveal individuality in a more or less carefully elected backdrop.

>Prickly drums pop the silence and startle the passengers. The driver's singing lags.

Le monde entier est un cactus
Il est impossible de s'assoir
Dans la vie, il y a qu'des cactus
Moi je me pique de le savoir
Aïe aïe aïe!
Ouille!
Aïe aïe aïe!

<But she doesn't register them.
<Anxiety is made of distance.
<Or maybe it's the opposite.
<Both besieged & barricaded with a sadist and its arsenal.
<Staring down the barrel of failed interactions & throbbing seconds & dapped tears & blunders & expletives & flushed cheeks & absorbed hits.
<Success & failures are both scraped by the coarse lining that makes up the anxious mind.
<At night, worries are fluffed up. Readied for insomnia.
<In the morning, flaxen rays reveal the purple crescents that underline the fatigued glazed eyes.
<But mostly, it's like being stuck interacting with the reality within your skull.
<All vicinity is made peripheral.

The bus chugs the last metres before her stop. Its doors unclench and the eyes of merry riders converge again.
A good day is bid.

Whistle While You Work

INT: SPACIOUS OFFICE BULLPEN
Staggered rows made of desks in which employees are encased,
assisted by docile screens & keyboards,
yoked by headsets,
steered by a software and,
last but not least,
bestridden by marketing.

Between two calls, as the fingers press words onto the screens, the eyes fall to the
bottom right corner of the screen.
2hrs left.
Earworms wiggle their way down to dancing fingers.
Come with me, little girl, on a magic carpet ride.

Logging back in.
Call – 10 min-no sale
Call – 1 min-no sale
iterations   like incantation produce   a trance like   state

Call – 2 min-no sale

Mental strands fold and unfold like party whistles

Call – 50 sec-no sale

navy cherry iris & black strands

Call – 1 min-no sale

she slobbers an army of tin soldiers unaware

Call – 30 sec-no sale

that death is slurping her brains through a plastic straw

Call – 4 min-no sale

twirls

Straw **slashing**

The striped **and stirring**

berry smoothie **the strands**

into a

Call – 25 min-no sale

Down her neck

The sunflowers of her white blouse

Call – 30 sec-no sale

shrivel

Call – 1 min-no sale

and are reborn

Call – 35 min-sale

as yellow chrysanthemums

Call – 1 min- no sale

eerily matching death's garland

Call – 13 min-no sale

Meanwhile

Call – 30 sec-no sale

The green of its peacock feather cloak grows more and more lurid.

Call – 3 min-no sale

Teeth on a bracelet clatter and glint.

Call – 22 min-sale

Call – 40 sec-no sale

The day is finally over.

Smirk

IN THE BACKGROUND: The cacophonic droning of calibrated conversations.

The ethically anemic guile of reluctant salespeople.

The sharp pop of privacy perforated by the tusks of capitalism

The century old scientific organisation of labour will attend our funerals and time it.

24

The Hum of the Assembly Grind

Roomies text chain:

Gab: ON MY WAY 2 WEEEEEERK.

2NIIIIIIIITE'S NITE!

11:11

Same building, different bullpen

Another squeezed head

tied to a computer.

       But not yoked.

Nora

—a single plait lost among auburn springs, her right hand fiddles with the pendant of

her necklace, brown blouse, black velvet vest with tassels, bell-bottom jeans, earrings

reminiscent of Gothic Rose Windows—

doesn't feel the urge to peel

the old mandarin clock.

The screen in front of her

is no mirror.

Her magpies' words

don't offend her.

Her train of thought may be transfixed right now;

its billowing steam gelled into a groovy beehive,

still this is all just an interactive experience,

like watching a spooky or romantic movie,

a borrowed timeline.

So, as far as she's concerned

the mandarin is worm-free

Roomies text chain:

Mo: SOME JERK'S EATING THE FOULEST SMELLING CHEESE ON EARTH

IN THE BREAK ROOM. TAKE THIS OUTSIDE, YOU FOOL! x)

12:12

Terrace of a restaurant:

a goldfinch lands on a tottering table.

It spastically observes Gab,

—Blank t-shirt, azure apron, black bell-bottom jeans,

silky black plait swinging like a pendulum—

while she empties an umpteenth ashtray

into the gaping mouth

that foams with jilted goods.

Tables are reborn with

fresh napkins, cutlery, plates

& the arrival of new patrons.

No birds in the bushes,

they're all pecking crumbs.

Gab is fumbling for hers,

jingling in her pocket.

Lunch is just starting.

The goldfinch has joined

the pigeons & blackbirds in

flossing the cobblestones.

The roles are reversed,

she is the one observing it,

even wishing she could hold

& pet it.

Roomies text chain:

Ash: DAMN IT GAB! I'M DRIVING AROUND SINGING WERK WERK
WERK…IT'S NOT OK. JK

13:13

A delivery van pulls up in front of an apartment building.

Ash

—white & blue tie-dye t-shirt, ripped jeans, green bandana, a green feather hangs
from the porthole in his left earlobe—

steps down & opens the sliding door of the van.

Picks up the parcel.

Rings the bell.

Earworm sings through his mouth.

While waiting he notices a Danish tallboy chest of drawers on the curb.

The door buzzes open. The parcel handed. Transaction over.

The black spores at the bottom look like lambrequin arches.

In this case, revolting yet magnificent.

He caresses the brass swan-neck handles.

Can't exactly take it home in the van, reckons Ash.

He's going to be late for his next delivery, but he just needs to know if all the drawers
are empty.

Gentle tug. The handle comes right off.

In fact, they all do.

Pitter-patter of sandals against the curb.

Jumps in the van. Plops his brass treasure on the passenger seat.

Roomies text chain:

Nora: THX FOR PAYING IT FORWARD ASH!

14:14

Stationery store,

Mo

—black clinging t-shirt, straight-cut jeans, floral converse, unakite stones around left wrist—

in low-key marketing mode. Secretly sampling materials for his own craft. His loot ironically stashed in the store's tote bag.

Velcro positioning that grabs the mind, and the money.

Guilt-free. He's a craft-pusher.

He's colourful. Aquarelle not gouache.

A flock of mavericks flip Dr Eckleburg the bird

as they walk into the store & it makes him, Mo, smile.

A customer asks where he can find crepe paper and stencils

The unakites of his bracelet jingle.

His lilt turns the most mundane words into arabesques.

phone shudders in his pocket.

Sleight of hand opens the phone case.

right: the screen, a conveyor belt of notifications

left: the card holder; visa card, a couple of loyalty cards & a King of Hearts—

a private joke between Mo, Gab, & Ash when they were tweens.

I'll pay by card. What do you mean it's not the right card?

Imagine their faces. All confused.

Since then, Mo's been carrying the King of Hearts,

Ash the Jack of Clubs,

& Gab the Ace of Spades.

Earshot

California by Joni Mitchell starts playing in Emma's earphones.

Nora: Hey, Em! Em! Em! Oy! Gently squeezes Emma's arm to get her attention

♪ *Sitting in a park in Paris France* ♪

Emma finally turns around: Hey, Nor! She takes one of her earphones out. Sorry… music for the bus, you know.

They keep walking and exit the building. Heading for the bus stop only a handful of meters away

♪ *Reading the news and it sure looks bad* ♪

Nora: Right. Chuckles Just wanted to know if you were still coming to the party tonight.

♪ *They won't give peace a chance* ♪

Emma: Shakes her head errr…yes. I mean…I'm kinda exhausted but…

♪ *That was just a dream some of us had* ♪

Nora: with a coaxing smile Oh come on! It'll be fun. Every time I invite you out for a drink you bail on me. She adds with an exaggerated pout. Not this time. It's my party. I'm gonna escort you there If I have to!

♪ *Still a lot of lands to see* ♪

Emma, contrite: I'm sorry. You're right. It's nothing against you though.

♪ *But I wouldn't want to stay here* ♪

Nora: I know. But tonight, you and I, we're finally having that drink together. End of story. Says calmly so as not to spook her conspicuously skittish colleague. They've now reached the crowded bus stop.

♪ It's too old and cold and settled in its ways here ♪

Emma: Ok. Chuckles awkwardly. Who's coming? What time?

♪ Oh but California

California I'm coming home ♪

Nora: 9. I'll text you the address. And, basically, everyone from work. Also, a few former colleagues turned friends.

♪ I'm going to see the folks I dig ♪

Emma: Wow. Clicking her fingers with her thumbs. Should I bring something?

♪ I'll even kiss a Sunset pig

California I'm coming home ♪

Nora: Yourself.

♪ I met a redneck on a Grecian isle

Who did the goat dance very well♪

Emma: I'll be there, I promise.

♪ He gave me back my smile ♪

Nora: No stomachache or headache this time?

♪ But he kept my camera to sell ♪

Emma: smiles with embarrassment.

♪ Oh the rogue the red red rogue

He cooked good omelettes and stews

And I might have stayed on with him there

But my heart cried out for you California ♪

The bus pulls up.

♪ Oh California I'm coming home ♪

Nora: Saved by the bus. See you in a bit then. À toute!

♪ Oh California I'm coming home♪

Emma: Yeah. Awkwardness draws a squiggly ketchup smile on her face.

♪ I'm your biggest fan

California I'm coming... ♪

Deflated Paper Buoy

Emma is sitting on the floor of her living-room, fully dressed.

Sandals buckled   leans back   palms to the floor.

Her eyes climb the wall in front of her, until they reach a sea of whimsically arranged photos. They usually buoy her, which is exactly what she needs at this moment.

Friends grinning. Posing places. Places & People she hasn't seen in months. Years sometimes. A congealed reality that won't thaw.

Flat. Hardened. Inaccessible.

Still, she gives it a try.

Concentrating on the pictures on the wall.

On

v
e
r
t
i
c
a
l
horizontal
v
e
r
t
i
c
a
l
horizontal
v
e
r
t
i
c
a
l
horizontal
v
e
r
t
i
c
a
l
horizontal

planks floating with an eerie stillness on a dead cerulean sea.
Projecting herself onto the first one.

Feeling her friend's cheek against hers.
The teen smell of foundation.
Picturing the dexterous hand of her friend
holding the camera just high enough
For them to look their best
& focusing on keeping her eyes open.
The punctuating flash, and the customary checks:
eyes open, blemishes unfortunately still there…
Damn, that nose.

Then she releases her hold and swims right to the next plank.

Euphoria surges as she takes in the picturesque mountains and
lakes. Completely and gratefully awe-struck. She can see the ink well in which
illustrious poets dipped their quill. Ephemeral friends are here somewhere. One is
taking the picture, but which one she can't recall. What remains is a giddy smile and
the grandiosity of nature. Staring out of the reverberating skull.

Releases, and swims to the next.

Agglutinated with other ephemeral friends.
Pints of various beers tower like skyscrapers
on the table in front of them. She can hear the
music. She can visualise their tensed eyes
and pleated brows as they comically attempt
to enunciate after a pint spiked by
the week's toll. Accents thickened while the English
language seemingly thinned out.

She releases and swims to the next.

Sitting cross-legged in the grass, legs and feet buried under the skirt of her medieval princess costume. 3 Pirates, a cat, 2 cheerleaders, a jedi, and a goth close the circle around a pile of chocolates & sweets & crisps & juice boxes & sodas & cookies. Right on the balmy threshold of spring. All jelly-faced. All fizzy. All acidulated & crunchy. All gorging before cramming. Celebrating the tasks behind and ahead. Staccato harmony. Just a couple of metres away. Just a few months away.

She releases the plank.

The water of the wall has hardened.

Vertical collapses into horizontal

Something like asphalt ensnares her body from the waist down. She reaches for the plank only to realise it's now a broken white line on a road. White paint has replaced the circumscribed past. She isn't trying to free herself though. In fact, she is simply looking around. Virtually roaming the boundless horizon. Cacti, succulents, and dahlias have grown from the saxe blue ground. They flank the road that tightly cups her.

Right in front of her, smackdab in the middle of the road, a spindly long-haired man, with a thick moustache & green aventurines for eyes. He is standing over a tall milk pail. Made of red steel. He brings the ladle—until now used for stirring—to his mouth. He gently blows on what looks like broth, before slurping it. He takes a rainbow bowl out of his tartan flannel shirt and unloads two full ladles in it. His eyes finally meet hers as he comes to hand her the bowl and a spoon—plucked from the other pocket of his shirt. They exchange friendly smiles as silent salutations. She submerges the big spoon in the broth. The spoon emerges with its oval head filled. A toothless, lipless mouth, as big as the head, opens and consumes the liquid. Once. Twice. Until it becomes absurd. But droll.

She spots something in the distance. It's rolling towards her.

A skateboard. With something on it. Something she can't quite make out just yet.

The sound of the wheels scraping the grainy asphalt is almost guttural. Like someone continually clearing their throat. Or gargling. Or throat singing. On the board, a chihuahua-size worm looks like it's stuck in a striped plastic straw ~~wearing a straw~~. It smirks. Or at least, that's what she thinks. It rolls before her, eclipsing her for a moment, then away. She catches her reflection in a nearby cactus. She gasps loudly at the sight of the disposable kodak camera that replaces her head.

On the coffee table, her phone vibrates, lighting up.

NORA: Don't! ;)

Emma chuckles.

She replies: **You're freaking me out! I'm on my way!**

She gets up, plucks her floral rucksack from the sofa, plugs her ears with her earphones and heads out.

In her ears:

> ♪ *On a night like this*
> *So glad you came around*
> *Hold on to me so tight*
> *And heat up some coffee grounds*
> *We got much to talk about*
> *And much to reminisce*
> *It sure is right*
>
> *On a night like this* ♪

Invisible Ink on Popping Petals

It's 7:30 at Nora's & her roomies. Nora is in the kitchen, standing over a yellow Formica table, while her roommate, Mo, is in the garden. Both are setting up for the party. *Mas Que Nada* throbs out of a beat-up speaker. Nora's hips and shoulders meet its rhythm. She is putting finger-foods on platters.

Coming in from the garden MO: Nor'!

NORA: Yeah? *Eyes down. Focusing on her task.*

Entering the kitchen MO: Did you pick up the juice?

NORA: It's in the fridge. *Still looking down as she buries the poppies of the platter under pigs in a blanket.*

MO, *opening the fridge*: Thx! *Takes out of the bottles of OJ, unscrews the lid and drinks from it.* So…how many for you? *Sits in a chair next to her. Looking up at her.* I invited like 20 people. Like old school friends that I haven't seen in a while. Cousins even. I dunno if they're all gonna show up though. Still, cleanup tomorrow is gonna be rough!

NORA, *finally looks at him*: Look at you, Mister popular! 6. All work related. Friends. Or friendly colleagues at least.

MO, *his left leg drills his foot into the floor*: How do you do it? I leave my colleagues when I leave work. That's where they belong. Our relationship I mean.

NORA, *empties a bag of crisps into the leaves of the chip & dip:* It's hard to meet people outside of work, you know? *Shrugs her shoulders.* You guys all have your own group of friends. I don't want to be, like, an interloper. Plus, they're nice.

On top of the kitchen cabinets, a colony of miniature elephants; made of wood, glass or ceramic, blow red and blue bubbles.

Some of the bubbles spastically morph into daisies plucked by an invisible hand playing *'she loves me. She loves me not.'*

The others stretch and thicken into bushy orange trees.

Not that they notice.

MO: Man…I'm sorry you feel that way. You're always welcome to join us. You know we like you, right? *Gently pokes her shoulder with his index finger.*

NORA, *Smiles and nods.*

Nat King Cole's version of It's Only a Paper Moon *comes on. Nora immediately starts bopping and swinging her head to the melody.*

MO: I guess, I don't even try to make friends at work cause I've got all my buddies here already. We've all grown up here. That makes me and my friends sorta smalltown…I guess sometimes we forget that you're new here. You've been here, what, a year?

NORA, *acquiesces.*

MO: You know, your friends can come visit. No problem! *Gestures for emphasis.*

On the wall on their right, the art nouveau motifs of the Biscuit Lefèvre poster suddenly stretch out of the frame. Creeping up and down the wall. Undulating.

The pastel colours erupt. Becoming almost luridly bright. Turning up the volume of the entire room.

Barring Nora & Mo.

Dimmed by subtext.

NORA: Thanks.

MO: Remember the first conversation we had? *Percussive laughter.* Saying the same thing and yet somehow having a fight. *Playing air piano with one hand.*

NORA, *chuckles*: And everyone was like 'you are saying the exact same thing' trying to calm us down. I could tell they were kinda nervous almost biting their nails, but it was just so nice to finally talk to a like-minded person. *Casts a brief but benign glance at him.*

MO, *runs his hand through his short curly hair*: Your face when you turned to Gab and said, 'yeah, we know'. She was so confused. *Nora starts to hum.* They really thought we were gonna strangle each other to death. I mean, to be fair, I don't usually get this worked up when I talk to people. I've been friends with Gab and Ash since we were 6 and they've literally never seen me that way.

NORA: I don't know if that's a bad thing or a good thing. *Organising the mini-quiches*

Their bloated words balloon.

In Fiddlesticks font.

Turning into pastis scented & opaque words. The curving words soar through the air. Or more accurately, drop & plop. Forming a puddle on the ceiling.

MO: Me neither. It probably doesn't have to be an either/or situation. *Nora turns around, goes to the sink to wash a bowl, and comes back.* Are you the same with all of your friends? *His eyes finally fall on the table.*

NORA: No, you're right. You're right. I just can't believe I met Gab before you. It doesn't feel like that now. We barely see each other anymore.

MO: Right? Your schedules haven't matched since you left the restaurant. She told me the other day, it's been, what, 4 months? She got bumped down because of it, she said. I'm your main friend now. *Nora is finally done with the food. She checks her clothes for stains. She is wearing light blue bell-bottom jeans and a brown blouse with orange spirals. She pulls her necklace out of her blouse. A brass compass slides down a dangling leather thread. Behind the iron needles, a yellow pansy substitute for the wind rose.*

NORA: Awww…I miss her. *Pulls the chair to finally sit down next to him. The dark chocolate of her irises at last mirrors his features.* By the way, where is she?

MO: Probs getting some stuff for the party with Ash. It's their thing. They show up late but with cool party favours. The next day they always do most of the tidying up though. They're cool like that.

NORA: Cool.

MO: By the way, do you need a hand? I'm done with the garden. Lights, tables, chairs, and all.

NORA: Na, I'm done. I'm gonna head upstairs for a minute. Probably shower and change.

MO: Alright then. *He smacks the table before getting up and leaving the room.*

Whirly Pop

Nora is sitting at her dressing-table. Her hands, like autumn maple leaves, lie flat against the wood's shades of dark brown. A garland of glossy memories adorns the mirror's rim. Her gaze teeters on the edge of the looking-glass.

Her tea whistles an anise air. She stirs the yellow water with the tea bag before taking it out of the cup. The tea briefly swirls, then returns to flat stillness. The swirling feels familiar, she reckons. Except, it's usually polychromatic.

Warm colours spiraling on her father's chest.

♪ *'Don't you want somebody to love? Don't you nEEd somebody to love? Wouldn't*

YOU love somebody to loooooooove?' ♪

Love was already his.

♪*'Elle ne porte rien*

 d'autre qu'un peu

D'essence de Guerlain

Dans les cheveux.' ♪

>Love: the auburn springs of her mother's hair.
>Love: the birthmark on her left elbow
like wine rings around the sharp bone.

>Raisin-like fingers played with a wedding band. Spinning it around the raisin finger<
>Her mother's curls fell down someone else's shoulders<
>Except white. Except shorter<

>Chanel No. 5 & Orange blossom. Moist & soft bark faces looked at her fondly<

>One paused to exhale smoke away from his granddaughter. Fanning it away.
Spinning it away<

>Her stomach had churned the night before. So had her mind<

>Churning a flurry of motley scenarios<

>Like the spinning colours of her father's shirt.

>Except, the colours had darkened with insomnia<

>The incandescent hotplates of the stove. Her mother's raffia mats. The purple smile
on her mother's face as she spun yarns. Cooking, or possibly the fragrance that came
with it, made her mother salivate souvenirs.

She brings the tea to her lips. She takes a sip of lemon balm, anise and levêche.

>Nora's felt tip pen slid on the page. Along the dented edges of the Spirograph's
stencil. Drawing a mandala within a mandala. While her mum's lilt coloured the
empty spaces with grandma's lavender silhouette and pansy hair. How both her
mother and grandmother loved gardening and reading. They were good friends. Until
it was time to cook dinner for grandpa. Ringing midnight on their fun. Turning
grandma into the dutiful matron. Peeling, chopping, and cooking dinner. Peeling,
chopping, and cooking her daughter to be 'proper'.

>Nora fiddled with the tassels of the tablecloth<

>Twisting them around the fingers of her left hand<

>When that failed to soothe her, she started plaiting them<

>Seasons swiftly passed in the cup of coffee in front of her<

>The biscuits by the cup read « un été » « je vous aime » and « tu rêves »<

>Her father's mother was there too<

>Leaning forward, forearms resting against the odourless roses<

>Closed<

>Latched<

>Barring an eye, which was pressed against the peephole<

Slightly muffled ♪*I went down to the mountain, I was drinking some wine*

I looked up into heaven, lord I saw a mighty sign

Writ in fire across the heaven, plain as black and white

Get prepared, there's gonna be a party tonight♪

Bubbling up from the living room

Except it's Friday night.

Except she didn't see no sign.

Except nothing about **this** is as plain as black and white. It's all shards of stained glass.

Dazed Dial

| A strobe-light | sequences | both | time | and | space |

| sequences | their | conversation |
| Nora |

| & Emma | are | on | the sofa |
| while | Ash |

| & Gab's friend | Neal | is | on |
| the floor | spiral |

| Eyed on | account of | the | taut & |
| spastic |

| light the | party's been raging | for |
| over |

| an hour | *Gab spiked the punch Have you* | *had some?* |

| Nora | & Emma shake | their heads |
| no. Neal |

indicates   the patio and   mimes drinking

Says *have some! Things'll be*   *wayyyyyyyy*   *more*
                fun then

And flops back down   Emma   reckons:
          it feels

like the   spoon like   the light
          is opening

and closing   its   mouth   and
          they're   sitting on

its   padded tongue   dumbstruck
dazzled   eaten

Ash has   joined Neal   on the floor   Speaking crumbs

They check up on him   his eyes are
                like darts

& the bullseye is the   clock   *STOP*
                          IT! STOP

STEALING   *TIME!* Nora slides down to
                the floor

to coax   Ash to get   up and
          leave   the room

<table>
<tr><td>He quickly</td><td>cooperates</td><td>&</td><td></td><td>as</td></tr>
<tr><td></td><td>she</td><td></td><td></td><td></td></tr>
</table>

<table>
<tr><td>helps Ash</td><td>walk out of the</td><td>room</td></tr>
<tr><td>she also</td><td></td><td></td></tr>
</table>

<table>
<tr><td>beckons Emma</td><td></td><td>who</td><td>leaps</td><td>off</td></tr>
<tr><td>the padded</td><td></td><td></td><td></td><td></td></tr>
</table>

<table>
<tr><td>tongue</td><td>&</td><td>follows Nora</td><td>out</td><td>of</td></tr>
<tr><td>the room</td><td></td><td></td><td></td><td></td></tr>
</table>

Peach Grooving

On the patio,

al fresco,

Emma & Nora

surrounded by revelers on a spectrum from

slightly tipsy   to   completely out

of their skulls.

The two women often snap a glimpse at the others as they come

tottering by,

        dancing by,

            zooming by

               or merely passing by.

They are both sitting, lotus position, on green bean bags with purple stripes.

Barely 2 meters apart.

        Facing each other.

Nora is wearing a Basque-red prairie style dress.

Her compass rests on her abdomen.

Her hands are a festival of gems.

Barring a silver San Cristobal medallion repurposed as a ring.

                    Emma is wearing a burgundy peasant skirt.

                        With a shy floral pattern.

                   An ivory Bardot top with puffy sleeves.

                        And a black cardigan.

                           Spartan.

The music from the living-room hobbles outside. It's mimed by people twisting their
way to the patio.

Kindred sartorial choices.

'I didn't mean to hound you.'

'You didn't.'

A silence akin to warm & honeyed milk.

The two women start swapping work anecdotes.

Work anecdotes as a receptacle for their tastes, quirks, & slices of their personalities.

One enjoys her earphone bubble while the other is into copiously chatty lunches.

One makes lemonade out of sour customers while the other winces.

One tunes the hassle out while the other embraces it.

One feels nicked by jagged days while the other feels merely tousled by the taunting week.

Both agree that

at times

it feels like

their skulls are ashtrays

with the stubs and ashes

of other people's

thoughts.

People flagging each other.

People flash themselves

      into digital memory.

Leaning back.

Eyes resting .

Between scrunched up pieces of tin foil.

Strewn across a navy satin & weirdly rippled cloth.

47

Voices strain & stretch.
The table with the pineapple punch bowl
on their left
& Gab
who has tasked herself with monitoring
the punch
is lying on the ground
her head and neck resting on an orange & purple bean bag
Hungrily eyeballing the sky
through sugar coated eyes.

Technicolour spills onto the grey cobblestones.

♪Clowns to the left of me
Jokers to the right
Here I am
Stuck in the middle with you ♪

People tongue-tasting each other
In the privacy of liquid lack of self-awareness.

Emma & Nora
in an alcove
ensconced
in a fuzzy peach
amid
a zany strawberry field.

Other similarities
Pickled problems
& Orchard thoughts
& moisturising hope
colour & music palettes.

Meticulous orchestrating and decorating has sanded the casual edges of the party.

That's what the hemp up is for.

That's what the pineapple punch bowl on the red picnic table is for.

To serve a pineapple glass of freewheeling.

Boisterous Mo   a green light about him

bears down on Nora.

Gobbles their peach

& plops down on Nora's lap.   The bean bag coughs

Exhilarated and zany,

he greets Emma

with the back of his floppy hand

& contorts his body

to give his seat a big grin.   They shiver from the stroke of a peppermint

wind

which lingers

melting into

a scorching & syrupy stare.

Red Lilies on full volume.   randy tinsels flicker

Without taking his eyes away from her,

he hitches up the puffy sleeves of his summer coloured shirt.

Nora perceives the fluffy & floral crooning.

Surprise jolts her gaze.

It runs through her

to Mo

who straightens up

& beacons the two to the table.   A very familiar score

for a glass of punch.

Crackling sound of a needle running out of grooves.

Citrus Parallels

INT: THE KITCHEN

Mo made of muslin & Nora – Commiserating wallpaper – Rounding Corners

Mo is sitting on the floor. Back against the wall. Next to the Biscuits Lefèvre poster.

The wallpaper is monroe bisque

With bouquets of popping lavender

Nora, back against the table, glass in hand,

facing Mo.

Superimposed lightning bolt splits the room in two

—Her side

His side—

The wall's lavender, swished by a copper wind, pats his back.

He brings his knees to his chin

to rest his head on the sky blue of his jeans

& wraps his frothy yellow-sleeved arms around his legs.

Believing he would be less diaphanous that way.

His left-wrist, heavy with foresight, falls to the floor.

The thread of his bracelet is bare

For stones have crumbled into coffee grounds

dying the room black.

Except for

in his eyeline: a mondrianesque glass partition,

grapefruit coloured.

The corners soften and the lines curve in front of him.

In the meantime, the lightning bolt gash closes

He smiles and says : Lemonade.

Pulpy & percussive pangs – A soulful brass gale – The crinkle of paper words

crunched up on still tongues

51

EXT: PATIO & GARDEN

Emma – A juicy Moon – A nonplussed sundial – A dangling & cringing necklace

She takes a sip from the pineapple glass

& slides down to the ground

until only her head is resting on the bean bag.

Both hands on her glass with fervor—as if to turn it into a votive candle.

In her eyeline: a bright slice of apple.

Hungry—hunger jolts her up.

Table – handful of food – crunch – chew – swallow & Repeat.

In her eyeline: something jutting out of the wall.

A fin? The wall has a fin?

Horseplay drives her away from the table.

In her eyeline: a set of uneven teeth hanging from a branch.

How come?

So hungry. Find food.

The order slinks from her mind to her feet.

Wahs set the contours of Night ablaze – the jabber is buzzing with paisley

whams – The knees of Night buckle – Night collapses with a static whimper

Super Realistic Slice of Time

Emma has suddenly decided to look for the end of the garden.

    A whim.

She saunters past the twinkling trees.

    Overblown broccolis to her.

Now it's just her and night.

    and night's tarp.

    or thick bedding.

Everything is tucked in.

She closes her eyes.

    Dots and blobs.

At least, with her eyes closed, she sees something.

She sits down, eyes closed.

Mark Rothko meets Jackson Pollock meets TV noise

on the inside of her eyelids.

Outside her eyelids, night veers off its course, like an out of control car, crashes into

day.

Lurid brightness rams its light into Emma's somber serenity.

The lids are pulled up, her pupils bloom and the pale light makes her squint.

Bits of fluff start falling from the occluded sky,

They feel wet, akin to drizzle.

Despite the white cotton sky, the light is a caramel cast on the scenery.

The feather light laughs of children tickle her attention.

She finds herself standing in the middle of a primary school,

Smackdab in the middle of its garden,

By a group of busy children.

They don't notice her.

They're tending to roses & other unidentified plants.

Their faces

are ringing

There she is

Her 8 year-old self

watering the roses and noisily chatting with her peers. The cared for roses happily

purr while the children discuss the unlikely possibility of being poisoned by the roses'

thorns & how they would need to find a cure, & maybe, the cure is something made

up of the other plants. Excited by the made-up drama, one of the boys pulls the

curtain up. His soft finger meets a thorn in a brief and harmless encounter, then,

looking at his intact finger, he proceeds to die, as loudly and dramatically as he can.

The other children gather around him and while he is wailing & jerking & moaning,

the others huddle up to remedy the situation. They make up the recipe. Duties are

assigned. They then disperse.

The roses look at this full throttle theatre with amusement. The boy's been quiet for

less than a minute when the others pretend pour the cure into his mouth.

"He's cured!" they cheer. Grownup Emma has been watching the whole time.

       Rivetted.

Watching the live theatre,

but mostly,

observing the flurry of emotional states that played out on her former features.

Shock, horror, determination, relief, and joy.

Emoting. Like a little thespian.

All while removing a nagging wisp of her curly hair off her bubble face.

& the colours,

Raspberry   Sunset   Peacock Teal   Lipstick

A five-pronged rake

gathering,

forming a heap

of maple-leaf-shaped

reel.

Commotion coming from the sheltered playground draws her attention away from the

children.

A horde of Rolex undertakers attired in Armani & Grey

zooming towards them,

deleting the chalk tick-tack-toes & hopscotches,

littering with:

Credit card & empty water bottles & candy wrappers & bills & razors & keys &

Valentine's day cards & steaks & phone chargers & plastic straws & tax returns &

twisted spoon & ticket stubs & brown bag & alliterative sound bites

A noiseless boom,

night siphons the light.

Siphons the school garden.

Siphons the plants.

Siphons the children.

Siphons the undertakers.

Siphons their rubbish.

All that the light contained.

It's pitch black in her skull.

Not a peep, tweet, or squeak.

So she walks on.

Determined to find the end of that never-ending garden.

The shimmying end.

Or is the shimmying beyond?

She passes Sheldon's room.

Through the window, she can see him.

Lying on a murphy bed.

Next to John Lennon.

Sitting on a stool by the bed, Samantha Stephens belts out Smelly Cat.

A second hushed explosion of light deploys its guile,

darkness is shoved away.

After a few seconds of adjusting, her eyes scan her surroundings.

Familiar street.

Yet she can't place it.

Not from the top shelf of her head.

Or is it top drawer?

Top something

Or

Top nothing?

Shops flank the street.

Looking around trying to identify the place.

Examining the storefronts of the different shops.

Each adjoined to another

&

 to another.

&

to another.

&

Again

&

 again

…

No end to the line of trees that flanks the road either.

The shaggy trees with clumps of leaves

Friendly fragrant trees. Lime and C.K.

They wear buttercups and poppy slippers.

A row of clocks of all shapes and colours adorns the storefronts.

Each clock is one minute ahead of the previous one.

11 to noon in a handful of meters.

The hands of the clocks are really spoons.

A big one and a small one—

scooping scraps of time away.

She keeps on walking.

Walking horizontally and vertically.

Cables & cogs lift her up & down.

11:01   Shaggy

11:02   trees

11:03   laugh

11:04   heartily

11:05   cranky

11:06   clocks

11:07   heckle

11:08   and

11:09   sneer

11:10

11:11   the trees

11:12   are bent

11:13   in two

11:14   in a fit

11:15   of hysterical

11:16   laughter &

11:17   tumble

11:18   forward

11:19   breaking

11:20   into socks

11:21   & underwear

11:22

11:23   a medieval

11:24   stand off

11:25   between

11:26   two grey

11:27   towers

11:28   4 pairs

11:29   of horses

11:30   blue

11:31   green

11:32   yellow

11:33   & red

11:34   drink

11:35	from
11:36	the salty
11:37	squares
11:38	
11:39	a storm
11:40	breaks
11:41	inside
11:42	the clocks
11:43	olive oil
11:44	winds
11:45	& chickpea
11:46	hale
11:47	& peals
11:48	of
11:49	breaking
11:50	bread
11:51	
11:52	the
11:53	upholstery
11:54	of her
11:55	mind
11:56	is made
11:57	with
11:58	silence
11:59	&
12:00	hunger

She abruptly stops,
her muscles stiffen with fright.
She turns around
& sees a giant mouth behind her.
Loudly munching and chomping the street into oblivion.

The mouth gallops

rapidly

toward her

in guttural gulps.

Emma starts sprinting as fast as she can

but the pavement has turned into a treadmill.

Despite her best efforts, she only moves backward.

The pungent stink of curdled milk stops her in her tracks

& a needle screeches pepper & tissues out of a vinyl.

The pavement has turned into stale bread

& the building have melted into milk—

the whole street crumbles

to be guzzled

by the green gummed

gluttonous mouth—

And a silent snap

rings out

honest & quiet darkness

ripples out.

Stupor trips Emma.

The earth under her is tender,

buttery,

brioche-like.

The mouth is gone.

In the distance,

the House

And its throbbing lights

Siren her

Night swaddles her back to tranquility.

Up

&

At

'em.

Darkness whooshes away again
And a colour infused light slowly descends
Only this time it's not bright

It doesn't blind her

It's a kaleidoscopic dance of patterns
Mandalas
waxing   and waning
followed by a spectacle of shapes,
all spinning randomly around
Hearts   Mickey's head   Dollars   Shamrocks   Upside down
triangles   Universal
Spades   The Nike logo   Arrows   Euros
        Circles   Embedded in circles   Hello Kitty head
Triangles   Hashtags   The Olympic circles   Stars

We can cast all of your hang-ups over the seaside
All fly about her
And like phoenixes,
vanish into death,   before being reborn.
A Day-Glo harlequin carpet softly sweeps her off her feet
Supine
back against the fabric,
contemplating
                pleasure   coloured   fireworks
springing from her
while the magic carpet goes on its ride

Have you ever been to
The sparks soar and burst into drooping flowers
popping
In   a   Gainsbourg   meets   Birkin
fashion
Her eyes fall from the sky
& meet familiar irises
who are lovingly looking down upon her.
Features mellow
She slides her arms away from her sides,
clockwise and counter-clockwise,

until her hands meet above her head

her arms forming a writhing halo

We can cast all of your hang-ups over the seaside

They know the melody, but are too immersed in each other to recognise it.

soundlessly panting and moaning.

Beads of onomatopoeia grow into bubbles

Day-Glo purple

rise & fall

from one bare skin

to the other

to be reabsorbed at last.

He kisses his way up her chest

meandering in the valley between her breasts

leaving transient kiss marks,

like footsteps from her navel to her neck

Until he finally reaches her lips

He moves back

Eyes meet eyes

& her subjectivity

& his subjectivity

became

their subjectivity.

I wanna show you

A Brain Freeze, Coppers & Squares

Ash is sitting on the kitchen floor.

Facing the fridge.

Curled up. Folded up.

Legs folded against his chest.

His veiled brow, green bandana, resting against his knees,

looking in

& enclosed by his arms. Squared.

The flickering clang of copper hooded eyes scalds the nape of his neck scarlet.

Their copper hooded eyes. Arrow slits.

He, their once crisp, now jilted, ticket to nowhere.

Glass pins keel over with a stained t-shirt sigh.

Robed up against the arrow slits. The copper hooded eyes.

Swaddled in a comfort that's really a noose around his neck.

Around his neck.

GASPS.

Ash uncurls & unfolds.

Ash is sitting up. Sitting back. Palms against the cold tiles.

Sweat darkens the emerald green of his bandana & buffets the paisley patterns.

He crawls to the fridge and opens it

the cold goes **SPLASH** against his red & swollen face.

He finds in front of him a barrier of Heineken bottles—

he grabs one

but before he has the time to do anything

the lid goes **POP** and a tiny spider crab crawls out of the bottle and back into the

fridge

where Ash's mum is setting the table.

Unfazed.

She doesn't see him

her not-yet-copper-hooded eyes are laser focused on the octopus on the silver platter

garnished with red corals.

The octopus extends one of its tentacles

and wraps it around Ash's waist,

like the rope of a robe,

and brings him in. Sets him on the cool platter.

He can't breathe under water. The red corals bleed copiously.

A retractable pen swims by. Clicking. Or possibly tutting.

Er. Why, what the fuck are you doing in there?

An iridescent & shimmering Gab approaches.

She takes his hands and pulls him out.

Dude, you know the drill, never alone. Never!

Next, he's sitting on a bean bag, on the patio.

I'm gonna get you a cuppa coffee.

Ash stares out into the garden

Flatly black yet patterned. Shimmering. Like an optical illusion.

You okay, mate?

The out of the blue voice jars Ash

Ash looks left where the voice is.

Former temp worker turned hip manager in a fledging startup company that specialises in turning rubbish into pricey furniture.

The man is square-shouldered and hipster-dressed. Ash is especially intrigued by his green silk vest, worn over a black t-shirt. Ash imagines the man standing beside him, currently sipping his brown drink through a metal straw, preening like a peacock in front of his mirror before coming to the party.

Why are you acting like we're friends?

No tottering. No trudging. The words crawl out sideways. & pinch sharply.

Ain't we?

Ash sees a Gillette ad in his beard & the metallic sheen of his ringed fingers.

You're such a fucking phony poser, man.

I had no idea you're a mean drunk.

Your beard is a fucking magpie's nest of shiny shit. You drink beer out of a fucking crystal pint. Fancy fuck. You're such a thin man.

Silence. The browbeaten man is hurt. Ash finally infers that the green of his vest is not peacock, but mallard.

You're just fucking bitter, mate. You're stuck between a rock and your own bullshit, so don't take it out on me.

He splits.

Gab is back with the coffee.

Ash stirs the sugar in. And licks the sweet silvery spoon.

Where do ducks go?

Plugged Brocade & Scoubidous

In the living-room
Strobe-light off   Kaleidoscope light on
Mo brings the top of his convertible mind down
                                  Eyelids down too
Watching the shape-shifting smudges & blobs & lines & squiggles
                                  in a reverse-projector way

                                  Taking in hitchhiking visions

****
Red dances circles around green
Green breaks into 4 yellow blobs
Yellow matures into orange
the blobs meld into a squiggly cross
Red shrinks & pales into pink
before bursting purple
& washing over
the other colours
from the outside
in
****

Leaning back on the sofa
Ash on his right
Gab on his left
Arms crossed
Gripping his flared sleeves

Dribs & drabs of pellicle
Open drawers with
– a protruding yellow protractor & a set square
– a stray glove compartment
– a graffitied school planner
– a bored rubber, disintegrated. Rubber scraps.
– a platoon of post-its off duty

****

Red dances circles around green
Green breaks into 4 yellow blobs
Yellow matures into orange
the blobs meld into a squiggly cross
Red shrinks & pales into pink
before bursting purple
& washing over
the other colours
from the outside
in
****

Mo

Gab

Ash

in

a

single

file

ritualistically

Tightrope

Walking

the

esoteric

Patterns

of

the

October

coloured

Rug

Wobbling

on

the

unplugged

Jacks

of

their

Pulp

in

Ash's

Living-room

****

Red dances circles around green
Green breaks into 4 yellow blobs
Yellow matures into orange
the blobs meld into a squiggly cross
Red shrinks & pales into pink
before bursting purple
& washing over
the other colours
from the outside
in
****

Gab   clovers   pansies
            tight
    sowing   and
buttercups
                    dandelions

    daisies   in their
        curls

A colour-coded origami crystal ball:
Blue: Playing   Red: Pick a
Yellow: fortune-teller   Green: Colour

1: Pick a number   2: To know your future
3: Rich
8: Fancy car
4: Famous
7: Children
        5: Married   6: Mansion

they
reciprocate
by
adorning
her
winding
plaits
with
the
patterns
&
plants
from
Gab's
gramp's
&
gram's
nose-catching
eye-tickling
mandala

****

Red dances circles around green
Green breaks into 4 yellow blobs
Yellow matures into orange
the blobs meld into a squiggly cross
Red shrinks & pales into pink
before bursting purple
& washing over
the other colours
from the outside
in
****

The old atlas in Mama's study
– when not distracted by the attention grabbing & dream-inducing Pink & Rose
William Morris on the walls –
– a synthesizer that's playing the tune but somehow you've got the keys –
the USSR one
the one
With the colour-coded countries
'Elmer the Patchwork world'

****

Red dances circles around green
Green breaks into 4 yellow blobs
Yellow matures into orange
the blobs meld into a squiggly cross
Red shrinks & pales into pink
before bursting purple
& washing over
the other colours
from the outside
in

****

Tripping on the Dark Geography of Light's Empire

Nora sets her untouched pineapple glass down on the kitchen table.
Mo has already left the room,
his brocade tuxedo & red lilies mirage, dissipated.
It's just her.

It's late, the week & the hour are adding up and taking their toll.
She feels her mind pushing on the pedals to power through,
only the wheels are stuck in couscous.

Across the room, the sink is brimming with glasses, serving trays, plates, a stray shoe,
and a condom wrapper.
South of the sink, where the mustard light doesn't seem to reach, a spider is trapped
under an Amora moutarde glass. In its own light. An empire within an empire
The upside-down glass reads 'Titeuf'. The illustration shows a little dude with a
single upward-reaching blond strand of hair.
Another reference that goes north of her head.
With her right hand she fiddles with her necklace.
Somehow, Ela & Abe's unison streams from the west of Time.

'If you miss the train I'm on
You will know that I am gone
You can hear the whistle blow
A hundred miles
A hundred miles
A hundred miles
A hundred miles
A hundred miles
You can hear the whistle blow
A hundred miles…'

She opens the cupboard west of her, gets a plain white mug out
& brews herself a cuppa coffee.

Coffee-ed up, arrow sharp and jangling with determination.
All around her, faces are illuminated from below by phones,
overhead lighting seems to fall short.
She looks for the 4 people she has in mind.
3 of them are vegetating on the sofa,
1 is wandering outside by herself

I'm taking you guys on a trip.

Book II:
The Citrus Circuit

Acoustic Brewing

Tick   goes Ash's watch

-             <Gab in a gnarly auditorium – a pea soup of faces – she is a vase of carnations>

Tick   <handing out the flowers to flannel squares – turtleneck hipsters >

-             <camouflaged patriots – mohawk-haired mavericks – blinged dreamers>

Tick   <the carnations grow from her throat up to her lips>

-             <smiling strangers with a handful of her voice>

Tick   <infinitely growing verse-speaking & cadence carrying carnations>

-             <Pixels of light dapple the black canvas of eyes suddenly less tightly shut>

Tick   Emma, Mo, Gab & Ash

-

Tick   Acapella performance by their surroundings

-             Emma — front seat — passenger side — resting against the window

Tick   Mo, Ash & Gab — a tetris of contorted upper bodies

-             Nora — empty driver seat

Tick   Gab <front booth – the top of Nora's friend's head>

-             <uneven soundbites fall down and dominoes snaps are arranged disorderly—most of them at least>

Tick   <hours & events shuffled in one crumbling deck>

-                                    <an electrified Mo beckons Ash & her into his room>

Tick   <a statement soaked like a napkin in sticky obscurity>

-                                    <jumble of thoughts & metaphors>   <Nora…a date with sunrise>

Tick   <cards, dominoes, & a smoking caterpillar>

-             <kill for coffee right about now>   harmonica warmth

Tick   *Guys, wake up!* she whispers, cushioned face & sleep voice

-             Doughy-eyed, Mo & Emma awaken

Tick   Ash stirs

-             *Ash*…she calls softly, strumming his hair – his green bandana coming loose

Tick   Her long plait caressing his bare arm

-       <rye — a field of rye — in his bedroom — childhood bedroom — and Ash
is not much higher than the rye — he reaches his bed — rugged black covers — Gab
is here — what is she saying? Her words bubble and burst against the muqarnas of his
skull>

Tick   Ash joins the waken world

-       *Where are we?*

Tick   *Nora's visiting her family & she invited us to join her* Mo explains,
speaking through a tobacco didgeridoo

-       The squeak of leather trumpets that Emma has joined the conversation

Tick   *Where did Nor' go?*

-       Shoulders shrug

Tick   Emma tries to peel the cellophane off of last night

-       <snatches of conservations & a folk song in a sizzling round>

Tick   the golden sequins of the preening Hummingbird clank

-       Gab steps out of the car

Tick   no coddling parking space

-       no bespectacled parking-meters   Dictaphone voices fade away

Tick   softly landing on grass

-       the gaping jean of her bell-bottoms cups her converse & the grass

Tick   around her : constellating daisies & dangling dandelions

-       lead up to a hassle-free hamlet

Tick   like a green enjambment   warm calendula petals shine

-       at the cusp

Tick   the kind of peace that lets you access anteroom thoughts

-       organ or flute playing exclamation points

Tick   grass   spring flowers   houses   a hamlet   weeds

-       Nora coming their way humming an unfamiliar air on thyme steam

Tick   a cup in each hand Nora beckons her friends out of their wooly haze

Zzuuuuuum goes, again, the omnipotent & omniscient rotary phone as its round dial
spins counter clockwise

Embroidered Denim-Tracks in the Prairies

Daylight casts lights & shadows from twin skylights
Through the twin stars of the stained-glass

Corduroy & carnivalesque introductions
Nora's parents, their Ikat, carnations or chintz, checkered, Harlequin & Escarapela
Rojo neighbours or friends & their children.

At Nora's folks. A converted barn.
Needlepoint, pyrography, carving, & painting. Patterns everywhere you look.
By contrast, the colour palette appears reined in: Rust – Turmeric – Basque red –
Hickory

Star-Dizzying Segue Sauce on a Time Tortilla
Four yolk-eyed strangers in a floral spare room.

Previously:

Hugs & gazanias & jackets on artful pegs complimented by a hickory frame studded
with flowers & *please sit down* & Moroccan tea set & *you must be beat* & the shaggy
tassels of the floor-lamp shade & unscheduled slivers of moonlight spice & tongues
like dry sponges & paisley & coasters for their question marks & tripping over the
motif lumps & caramelised blue circles & stirring through revolving doors & onion
rings of the mind sting the eyes & paisley everywhere & two paisley clad sofa facing
one another & turmeric ottoman & paisley words & paisley concern & what's not
paisley is the afghan handed to Mo who is shivering & not paisley is Nora's dad *call
me Abe's* brown peg trousers & white t-shirt or Nora's mum *Ela* burgundy maxi dress
Or the damask carpet. Still, the waft coming from the turntable spells paisley.
Turn! Turn! Turn!
Neighbours bring mattresses over. In the spare room: drawings, spools of thread, a
few stray knitting needles, a lonely cup, books, crayons & crunched up pieces of
paper, gestating rainbow reams & a blue & burgundy smock are scooped up or swept
to one side of the room. The mattresses flop onto the linoleum floor & are squeezed
into snug chintz or toile sheets.
Four yolk-eyed strangers
wrapped

The No Longer Sanded Amps of the Ampersand
A little R&R from the splintering Identity splits.
Relief makes her parents' lilts seesaw—their conclusion is just their warning on
repeat.
You can only hitchhike outside the lines of someone else's value for so long.
They couldn't, and probably still can't, see her in the rearview mirror, hitching a ride.
Prophesying from a transparent & projecting ball of recollections.
Nora knows what they're thinking. It's the sharp end of her principles that led her
back here.
When, in truth, Nora has been at the wheel since last night.
Needling the not-privy with the lime sting of immersion.

Excavating the Homesick's Blues

Paperback tongues have been flicking at the Foreign Four for a couple of days now. Some seem to be downright speaking in tongues. Ideological jargon.

Dig it?   Yeah, we get it.   No, roll up your sleeves. It's not getting.

From the frozen clock tower—both hands taking an endless drag on 4—they see a fenceless & gateless creedscape. Down to the wealth of tables—scattered across the place for spontaneous congregating—to the potluck amphitheatre or the trainless train tracks.

The tracks resemble a fallen ladder. Rungs of wildflowers & beads & pansies & ribbons & thyme & carnations & rosemary. The grown offerings highlight the tracks like a quote on a page. They haven't finished the book yet. They're reading its geography. Its iconography

They also visit a sanguine bus. A metal kitty—different feline, same spots— fossilizing in the grass. On its ribs, the visual of the bubble-gum mind of the frozen clock tower. Taxidermy. The seats are there, albeit gutted of their purpose. Rigor mortis. Revered.

An Organic Handful Just Left of Hayden

EXT: AMPHITHEATRE
Nora & the Foreign Four on the cupping hand of democracy
In the palm. By the monitoring stool.
They look into a small oak chest: tin whistle, castanets, maracas, djembe, tambourine,
harmonica.
This is what we call the Pop Pot; where we cook-up plans and projects for our
community. We meet here at least once a week. Everyone shows up. Have to. It's
mandatory. As soon as you turn 12.
Nora leads them to the sheltered seats. Up. To the last ring. The cupping fingers
Nora brings her hand up. Flat. Palm up. Yet still amulet-like. She presents the
words—ingredients—singed into the wood panels.

Principles
-Compassion-
-Solidarity-
-Equality-
-Coalition-

Prerogatives
-Food-
-Shelter-
-Well-being-
-Community-

Yep…You could say it's our motto. Our mantra even.

About our prerogatives…not as stingy as in most places. If you think of happiness as a destination then these actually give you a decent lift. Shelter & food are covered in the form of a house and a garden. It helps that we trade too. Barter more like. Ok…Man…I got sidetracked there. The Pop Pot! So…there's a different ref every week. The person goes through a list of topics, sometimes grievances, and we talk it out. I know it sounds like there's probably a feeling stick going 'round, but it's not that hippy-dippy. I mean we are reminded to be empathetic at all times, but it's mostly about the arguments & compromising. It all boils down to that. To living up to the values we set some 30 something years ago. People still try to get their way sometimes. It takes people like my parents, who never, or at least very rarely, have any skin in the arguments, to remind everyone why they are here in the first place.

Nora speaks with her whole body.

Not in a waving-a-placard-&-stomping way.

In a democracy-can-have-the-bad-breath-of-politics-so-here's-a-mint kind of way.

Her compass flaps and swings.

Resembling a pendulum. Set against a crochet firework display.

The 4:

Gab

—who is wearing a grenadine-pink carnation choker, courtesy of Abe—

takes in the almost dioramic words of the genesis:

Commune – spelt in rainbow dots

to **Community** – embedded in the rainbow.

Ash

is sitting cross-legged by the oak chest.

His beaded headband hides pondering lines.

Shaking a maraca with one hand &

reading the palm of this particular democracy with the other.

Mo & Emma

still up there. Keenly perusing the ringed fingers.

Mo, puzzled, admires the words on the wall

As if they were arcane symbols—intricate yeseria enigmas.

Awestruck by a society that's not pentimento-esque

or

palimpsestic

no redacted images, lines, or colours.

The obvious benefits of being on the lighter side of history's seesaw.

Nora is alphabet-soup spade-feeding Emma

who can't fathom

the absence of mealy-mouthed, marketing packaged incense & essential oil covered

buzzwords

No ad-lib, mad-libs, lip-service, or lament mongering

Not even curlicues of self-aggrandizing incantations

Just your good old in-the-kitchen-drawer-written-in-blue-pen-&-slightly-crunched-

up-family paradigm-recipe passed down from one generation to the next

People are not the vegetabilised ingredients though.

No carrot-eyed couch potatoes with mass-slaughtered ambitions.

No phony & pavlovian eat-your-greens with cannibalistic ketchup.

In all fairness
the hand is still covering their faces
they're only peeking through finger slits

A Rainbow of Loading Irises & Cough Syrup Phoniness & Clipped Musings & Itchy-Sideburns Reality

Emma is still effervescent. Despite the smooth-chinned context. Like aspirin dissolving in water. The scrunchie that keeps her taut doesn't slacken. Her hair is down only in appearance. Mind & body are girdled in

<I'm gonna get sacked…how the fuck am I gonna make rent? How come they don't care? I can't afford not to care>

On the flip side of the can of worries,

there's Emma, the people pleaser

She curls her mouth into a smile, curls her anxiety into laughs, curls her frustrations into nods…until finally naked under the shower head. Her hair pinned down by the white noise of water & naked & mirror & hate & she curls her hands into magpies… pecking at her thighs.

Release.

Slackening.

Dissolved.

Stuck in the itchy sideburns.

Discrepancies can be like fluff stuck in a zipper.

Ash's mind zips anyway.

Easy-going, easy-zipping.

Happily doing without the drowsiness induced by cough syrup phoniness.

<They dig objects. Dote even. The humility of the living, of the mortal, in the face of the timeless. Hoping their soul & story would rub off on them. Not in a *Dark Lord* kinda way. Not defying death. Compromising. Not factoring in the phony, wet, sleazy plastic-piss-cup clang in a or the phony green masturbation that usually pollutes objects>

Back home doesn't zip. Too much fluff.

Gab has been tuning up. Her distended irises are slowly shrinking back to their normal size. She is only now starting to chime in. It all resonates with her. Albeit with some reverberations & feedback <why so closed-off? So secluded? Why is it that only a lucky few get to live this way?> She's seen so many eyes with shriveled irises…both parched & drenched…that could have spared. People whose pupils were pebbles.

<Why do others have to whistle through gritted teeth when they get to belt out their own tune? Why do others have to resign themselves to be shriveled or pebble-eyed?> The reasons are simple enough. Mass dilutes principles. Mass tugs at compromise until its elasticity is shot. Consensus is a table & you need enough seats for everyone. &, last but not least, the resigned only belch cynical scoffs & grumbles *that's not life, that's eating strawberry pie on a plate of clouds.*

Mo has clipped & tacked snapshots to his mental foam board. The votive candles on the wooden train tracks. Raï steam billows from a Moroccan tea set. Bouquets of thyme, rosemary, anise, & mint. *¿Qué voy a hacer? Je ne sais pas ¿Qué voy a hacer? Je ne sais plus ¿Qué voy a hacer? Je suis perdu ¿Qué horas son, mi corazón?* A neon Peplum top that screams MTV, framed with 80s neon print. Wicker handbags hovering over peasant skirts. Art Nouveau bowed windows on a pastel blue day. The whirl of Druid concoctions. Fat-bottomed TVs. The unblinking eye on the peacock feather that adorns so many of the third-eyed fedoras.

All prisms. Nora stands at the receiving end of their rainbow. She plaits it into her hair.

Tugging at the Wooden Neck Sticking Out of the Rear-view Mirror of the Lemon Licked Charabanc

First stop: *Discarded Rollers, Sprayed on or Doodled Pompadours*

Mo's visiting the fossilised bus—part museum, part sanctuary, part sepulchre

Tokens or trinkets: pictures, watches, aprons, petticoat-ruffles, rings, grey-flannel suits, badges, uniforms, dog-tags…akin to clipped nails, peeled skin, & outgrown clothes

A catalogue of: newspaper clippings, posters, pamphlets, & flyers from love-ins, concerts, demonstrations.

Easily boxed-up hours spent dreaming, hoping, raging…that are nonetheless, non-refundable.

Up on the ceiling: sprayed strands of citrus minds—curl and unfurl.

Behind the flabby seats: doodles, quotes, lovers mathematically tied…

All of it reminiscent of the sordid glory of bathroom stalls & the freeing aura of public degradation.

The iconography of the iconoclast.

Mo runs into Coms (denizens): Hab & Rob:

Hab, Leica in hand, sporadically sprays the bus with white light.

Rob by his side for feedback.

All three are sitting around one of the lucky pennies.

Turns out Hab & Rob,

respectively

greaser visuals & beatnik words,

respectively

born here & moved here as a teen,

are both working on an exhibit.

Pairing the pictures with testimonies from members of the Community

Mo elevator-pitches his resumé.

Rob & Hab dig him—Mo's in.

They invite him over. Hab's got something in mind:

"Here's a polaroid camera, and if you could just take a few pics here and there of

things that stand out to you it'd be neat. I think it'd be wild to see with your eyes."

Nudging pieces of advice given.

Feed & bio info traded.

Mo is off with his third eye.

Second stop: *Carpeted Conversation & Comb-Over Carnations*

Mo sprays light on to a moment. Strong-hold light.

From left to right:

Ela, Gab, Nora, Kar, Abe

at Ela's & Abe's House—known as the O's house.

Nora & Gab are helping Abe make flower-jewelry

Ela has been giving a lesson on the Latin root of Romance Language to Kar. Which is

now over. Kar, like Nora, was born & raised in the Community of parents who laid

the ideological brick.

All in various states of sitting. All on the damask rug—the teapot & cups on the

coffee table.

Kar has her fabric-made folder with Kandinsky-like patterns in one hand—

Concentric spirituality & eccentric colours anachronically pulsing with 80s

rock *Taaaaaaaake me on! Take on me!* Black circles adorn her knuckles—mysticism.

Wooden beads hang on her short, curly hair—natural. She also sports a wooden

amulet. Square, but loopy angles. Crescent moon and a star carved into it—and holds

Nora's hand with the other hand.

Nora's necklace jangles, but that's muted by the spray.

How have you been? It feels like 50 carousel-rides ago.

What is that? Like an inside joke?

Yeah...a long long time ago, a fair came to the Community for the first time.

We were something like 8 or 9.

Yeah, we were dying to go on the carousel and were ecstatic when we finally got to.

But our expectations of the speed were...

Were so off. We kept saying our hair would be all like straight, you know horizontal,

flying from the speed like in a cartoon, she chuckles, *and in the end it was so slow*

that we spent the entire ride approximating how long it was taking us to come full

circle.

It became a whole bit. We were growing old because of how freakishly slow it was.

It became a whole thing. We decide that a ride was about a year.

We should have measured time in revolutions that would have made more sense!

Come on, we were little.

Ela's eyes are on her daughter & so are Abe's.

The spray holds their melancholy-crusted looks, nostalgia-stuffed smiles &

loneliness-clenched jaws.

But not the mint's octopus-like hold on this huddled lot.

Its misty tentacles have wriggled out of its teapot body & swelled around them.

Gab is still wearing her new carnation choker

which has faded;

grenadine-pink has gone yolk-yellow

due to the vandalism of bad vibrations.

Strung out vocal chords

like wallpaper yellowed by cigarette smoke.

Third stop: *Dug Up Honeycomb*

Mo points his aerosol towards the Pop Pot

& out it comes

Looking like

An onion democracy

Or a target?

the chair as a dart in the bullseye

Flaxen wood panels stilled into sand. Depth flattened
& yet, archaeologically & artistically deepened.
Looking down the rubbles of a Greek rib cage,
or maybe they're embedded citrus rinds. From the Pomelo right down to the
Kumquat.
The artistic blur spins the ancient into an optical illusion:

blank mandala

collapsible spyglass

lens

ripples

Encompassing yet ensconced
Rings ebbing into the earth
Or surging out

Or both

Fourth stop: *A macaroni-Framed, Banged Up Beehive*
Mo, egged on by convexing musings, spots Emma & Ash on his way to the train
tracks.
They're below eye-level. Shrunken.
Sitting down on the asphalt—deadpan ground
embellished by a chalk orchestra.

Bird's eye view:

Bongos & steel drums & djembes & tambourines & gongs & French horns & all
kinds of flutes & horns forming a semi-circle in front of a conductor.

The artist: Jam', has placed herself in the audience. Her hoop-earrings look like
chopped lotus roots. Her hands are still tangled in the pastel-coloured tape.

Ppsssshhhhhhhh!

Emma's pounding one of the purple djembes while Ash karate chops the orange
bongos.
Emma's cardigan is off, thus revealing a coin-sized coffee birthmark on her left
shoulder
Ash's head is finally bandana or headband free, thus revealing a smudgy cookie-sized
strawberry birthmark on his right temple.

Both :
On the lam, in a percussive and cabalistic cab
features are rounded in a rye & barefoot haze
harkening back to cereal sunrises.

The spray cannot hold:

The chanting

*"Carpe diem Carpe diem Carpe diem Carpe diem Sing
cuckoo sing Death is a comin' in Sing cuckoo sing Death is a
comin' in Death is a comin' in Death is a comin' in Death is a
comin' in Death is a comin' in Carpe diem Carpe diem
Carpe diem Carpe diem Sing children sing Death is a
comin' in
Sing children sing Death is a comin' in You can't outthink the angel of
death Sing cuckoo sing You can't outdrink the angel of death Sing cuckoo
sing Death is a comin' in Death is a comin' in Death is a comin' in
Death is a comin' in Sing children sing Sing children sing Sing
children sing Sing children sing…"*

The kinetic wiggling of the tapes &, consequently, the blurring of the instruments
outlines.

Ticker tape synapses & zip-lining ooooooooooooing onomatopoeia

Before winding back around the artist's hands

Reeled.

Fifth Stop: *Rosemary-Studded French-Plait*

Mo walks along the train tracks

His gaze combs through the post make-over carcass,

like turning a radio receiver into a box or a vase.

He comes closer to make out the singed words on the railroad ties:

  Goodbyes & Addio & Adioses & Adieus & Wadaeaan & Adeus

Letters to nowhere.

Planks at the bottom of the grass.

Rosemary's pneumatic memory curtailed

by marble stressed epitaphs.

Ppsssshhhhhhhh!
The camera does see that
it all resembles a severed guitar neck
frets begging for the pressures of fingers & strings
for the good vibrations
it also sees
the field bindweeds for what they really are
crumpled up tissues

Stepping down: *Swivelling Down the Rosette*
At Luciana & Sara's,
where Mo is now staying,
currently taking a soft-spoken self-portrait
Reframed
Bathed
Peeled
Combed
Transferred
Onto lavender Canson paper
A clamshell portrait
The page split in 2 by serpentine lines

On the left side
erotic
albeit
pent-up
Art Nouveau
undulating lines
&
A crescent
but bulging
moon
Sexual overtones
& undertones
Or just
A repository

On the right side
A reproduction
of the concentric arabesques he'd
avidly & reverently
Gape at
in soul-stirring wonder
swathed in a mint harmony
&
clove oneness
&
cumin patterns
&
orange blossom

his juncture is punctured by *Road to Nowhere* playing in the kitchen
where Lu & Sara are cooking.
The self-portrait goes on the desk
next to a grid of polaroid pictures.
extolling/undercutting there's no telling: eyes bring most of the colour.
An unearthed patchwork or storyboard, he hasn't decided yet
he wistfully spins his bracelet around his wrist.
His asymmetrical sleeves twirl like black calla lilies

Mo finds night's stubble itchy
But it doesn't derail his train of thought

The Strobe Light Song of the Troubadour

The whisked Foreign Four have been here for over two weeks now.

Nora has finally come clean to her sounding board. Her sounding band.
Their sound is punk, but the gist is clear: not monolithic.

Unlikely pairings are brewing—Gab & Kar and Ash & Em—unexpected answers:

Holed-up Kar realises that she isn't really *digging*…not using an empirical shovel
anyway.

Sword-swallower Gab removes the blades to let the carnations out…singing for the
first time in years…looking at pointless from a different angle.

The Dude Ash stops chomping rye or straw and unboxes the beauty he's gleaned over
time.

Emma's effervescent fog is watered-down or oranged-up, connection shrinks
anxiety's distance.

Mo has joined Nora in her figurative figuring out-room.
Being privy to a life not arched by stomping little boxes has turned his claustrophobic
clock into a sundial.

Outta Sight

His words crunch like pepper.

They consume his meaning like an artichoke, leaf by leaf, until they reach the heart.

All of it is somehow bolstered by the olive oil & tomato chant rising from his toast.

All I can say is that that 'freedom' was not for me. Its confines were too damn cramped. Like a cluttered and narrow maze. I tell you, it's the excess that's lauded and branded as 'choice'. The excess that hovers just outta reach. The same excess that you end up mistaking for access. Or for a shortcut. Or the path altogether. And you know what? Maybe it is, for some, I can only speak for myself, and I don't know how it's treated you, but it certainly wasn't for me. I was moving through the maze, and I swear I only found that the lower shelves had less and less to offer. And the high shelves reached new heights. Virtually out of sight. I swear to you. It all felt mighty outta reach. I blamed myself for my failing sense of direction. For not being able to envision a future for myself and wasting my so-called freedom.

Takes a bite of the toast. Chews. Swallows.

Capitalising. Quantifying. Calibrating. I don't know about you, but it wasn't, isn't, my bag. Numbers scared the shit out of me. Dyscalculia they called it. Not that I disagree. But I still remember how strongly I hated that dark blue rough book...buried under peelings of consumption in a drawer of my dad's desk. They'd bring it out about once every two weeks. They, as in my parents, would pore over it, in the kitchen, right next to my room and of course I'd hear them. Speaking numbers and expenditures. Mapping out the next few weeks. 'Told you to turn left.' 'Told you to choose a cheaper brand.' That's how I came to realise that they too were moving through the maze.

*My father was a mechanic and man did he dig his job. The smile on his face when he worked on a car...I tell you, he loved it. But my mother made these shitty jokes at his expense, especially when my grandmother and my aunt were around, like that she wished she'd married an engineer. Something his own parents had pushed for when he was in school except he had no love or patience for school. Neither did I, frankly. Looking back, I was a lot like him. Anyway, once he cut their usual bit by saying he wished **he'd** married an engineer too. Shut everyone right up. My mother was not that bad though. She did look for work, but it wasn't easy. I remember helping her time her typing. Sitting next to her, where daddy sat when they hovered over that goddamn dark blue rough book, and learning how to break down my life into taglines and numbers to make it look appealing. You know, like window-dressing. Can't tell you how depressed the whole process made me. And I remember wondering, right there, as we sat at my father's desk: But who's looking? Why can't we see them?*
'You have to learn to deal with this,' she said, 'it's just life.'

Takes a bite of the toast. Chews. Swallows.

It's just life. Groping through the maze while entertaining Doctor T.J. Eckleburg.

Takes a bite of the toast. Chews. Swallows.

What a joke! 'Don't take stock or push back.' Be harried without harissa. A balloon, eager to sore, yet tied to a dark blue rough book...

Takes a bite of the toast. Chews. Swallows.

Yeah, I spent a mighty big chunk of my years under the impression that I was weak. Unable to deal with 'life'. It looked like chewed up fingertips and darkly underlined eyes. The days were so heavy, or maybe I was just so damn weak, that it felt like they were pressing me down into the earth. I was told that I had no drive, no ambition. Mostly cause I didn't have dough on the brain. They made me feel like…like…like a damn wet pile of laundry. Like they'd put me on their clothesline and I'd flail in the wind. You know, pinned to the wire. Flapping. Getting tangled. Buffeted. But still, somehow attached.

Takes a bite of the toast. Chews. Swallows.

Then, randomly, I was driving around to calm myself down before a job interview, a paper pushing job, which wasn't my bag but my mum's friend had gotten me the interview so…anyhow, I parked my Renault 5 and went into the nearest café. Ordered some tea to, you know, to calm the old nerves. Sat down to relax. A group of people were chatting a couple of tables away behind me. Out of sight, but not out of earshot. They were toasting to a new life. 'Away from capitalism's commodification.' I remember the smells and words so distinctly. Twinned almost. Blackcurrant, 'pioneers', red wine, 'fenceless', anise, 'participatory democracy', orange, 'mellow'. My ears syphoned every word. I ended up blowing off the interview and ordering a coffee to pass the time. I remember blocking out the lyrics of Un autre monde. *My eyes perused the replica of the mosaic which lived in the train station, a few metres away. Staring at the colourful sails, the majestic ships and their shimmering reflections in the water. But mostly the frame. The alternating pattern that brought the vista together. Until finally they paid and headed out. When the door shut behind them I sprang up. Dropped the coin onto the bill tray. On my way out, I noticed that the tear-off calendar still said March 20th when the lilies of the valley around me clearly said otherwise.*

Last bite of the toast. Chews. Swallows. Rubs hands together.

Like I've been saying, I had been mining for some meaning. Searching for some sense of belonging. And there they were. Like-minded subterraneans walking above ground. Getting away from me and on a bus to build paradise.
'Wait!' I called out.

And that's when I met Nora's parents. Ela was wearing the necklace Nora's wearing right now. Kar's parents were there and so were Hab's. And Sal, Lu, Bets, Tom, Mal, and many more. Jamala was only an itty bitty thing then. There and then I joined them. Abandoned my beloved Renault 5 to get on that bus with people who looked mighty out of time. Paisley stuff, long-hair, flair-cut jeans. It was the 80s mind you. Such a different time. Anyway, snap decision. Off I was, with these people I didn't know from Adam. To a place I had only envisioned but never seen.

What about your folks?

I wrote them a long, and slightly rambling, letter. To say they were on the fence would be understating it. The word cult was used. I was 19 and the others were in their late 20s early 30s. Can't blame them for thinking they could smell a rat, right? Still, they came. Yeah, they did come, but only to add a visual to the already pre-established narrative in their mind. Although, even they had to admit it all seemed innocent enough. They've come around though. I know they don't dig it. But they've accepted it.

Takes a long sip of OJ.

We've built almost everything here from scratch. It was back-breaking work. But...Oh man...the sense of purpose. I was not wandering in the dark anymore. And, we were, still are, far from abundance. There were new limitations. New sacrifices. Honestly, I still miss some stuff like...going to the movies or being part of a crowd during a national event. All clapping as one at the end of 14 Juillet. Hearing the neighbours yell their heads off because we scored a goal. We. But I'm part of a smaller and tighter 'we' everyday here. And that moderation. That lack of abundance, or excess, is the absence of the very clutter that made the maze. For me at least. Now I can feel my own sense of purpose and freedom. Not only that, I can see it.

Chugs the rest of the OJ.

César wipes the crumbs off the table, to his hand & back to the empty plate before him.

Mo, Ash, Gab, and Em are sated.
And, in a different way, so are Nor & Kar & Hab & Rob.

Ticking Thyme & A Rosemary Scoubidou & Mint Dynamics

Abe, Ela, and Nora are sitting by the floral train tracks: Pansies & Yarrows & Mint &
Carnations & Oregano & Rosemary & Thyme & Wildflowers.
The tracks seem to either bypass the seasons
or to contain them all.
The wild thyme ticks, garnering everything from early coos to the late, solemn hearse
silence.

       The noon tangerine limelight is olive oil thick. But conditioner rinseable.

Abe is plaiting cuff from daisy fleabane.
Ela is plaiting Nora's hair into a halo.
Nora's stitching a spiral scoubidou.

       All three are playing conversational pelota.

You have my hair. Abe, doesn't she have my hair?

               Since day 1.

       Your mother's hair too.

Mint telepathy connects Abe & Ela.

Ela massages the sharp bone of her circled elbow.

Is that your not so subtle way of saying you've met your grandparents then?

Yes. All of them.

Nora loops 2 orange threads while

threads of rosemary needle Nora's memories.

She tells them about the turmeric tassels hanging from the tablecloth, the fans, the

copper pans, the geraniums, the chili pepper garland, the bougainvillea, porcelain

Virgin Mary, the droning commentary of a football game, & the gazanias.

She threads the 2 red & 2 purple into the loops.

The framed christenings, weddings, Easters, Christmases with unknown faces but

familiar features.

Finding out that dad got his sense of style and hairline from grandpa Omar and his

rounded nose & curly hair from grandma Miriam.

That mum got her long fingers and almond eyes from grandma Maria but the shape of

her face was all grandpa Louis.

And now it's hers.

She pulls the threads and tightens them into a knot.

Rosemary is threading Abe & Ela's memory too.

Adorning it with pansies

a whiff of aloe.

But the whole thing's rugged kiwi skin.

Like the skin of Ela's arms

as she scratches a somatic itch.

We met at your parents', mum.

As you can imagine, everyone was very tense at first

there was a moment of overwhelming silence

when you could hear a fly buzz by. Easily.

But then your mum, mum. I mean Maria. Asked about you two.

I told her you were alright. Happy. Then Dad's dad said,

'It's nice to hear that they're living a happy life away from us.'

To which grandma Miriam replied that he was aiming at the wrong target.

She then asked about me. About my life, and

they all listened politely as I rambled on about myself.

Finally I told grandpa Omar, all of them really, that I had come to understand

their side of things too.

Abe has almost finished the cuff.

You could have just asked us. We would have told you what they were going to

say.

Ela, still sporadically scratching her arm, lightly tugs at the auburn plaits to loosen it
up.

You know that's not the point though.

Frankly, I don't know what you were hoping for. You took the cast off when
everyone knew the limb was still broken, *cielo*.

I don't think this image applies to this situation.

Or maybe it's just not how *I* look at it.

How do you see it?

As she tightens yet another knot, she looks over her shoulder at her dad.

Distance. You know. Kinda like those tracks…

Time has stretched the tracks between you.

***Cielo*, it's not that simple. The wounds have been licked raw by now.**

She wraps the two plaits around her daughter's head & secures it with bobby pins.

Her halo glows with artificiality of phosphorescent light.

Maybe. But honestly, it's not just about you.

Thyme rattles the rungs of the fallen ladder.

After a doomed attempt to strum the stringless guitar neck.

Zinnias sprout, bloom & adorn Nora's halo.

Abe hands the daisy cuff to Nora & picks one of the zinnias up.

Nora loops to orange threads.

Thyme's scent finally undermines its tick.

She tells them about hearing her name in a stranger's mouth, someone slurring her
last name for the time, or reading it next to someone's else first name, or, simply,
having to state it, because people don't already know who she is.

She threads the 2 red & 2 purple into the loops.

About having to introduce herself and be her own advocate during a job interview.

About the self-asserting & self-affirming power of wrangling.

And how her own mind revealed itself to her.

She pulls the threads and tightens them into a knot.

The cuff, woven stiff & heavy, loosens & lightens to become a bracelet. Form
following feelings kinda way.

Nora's halo fades
or more accurately
becomes iridescent.

All the while, tentacle-less mint imbues the current silence, which can be mistaken for
distance, with the porosity of empathy .

Thyme's tick mellows into a thrum
appeased by Rosemary
& lulled by the tangerine light.

A Handless Bullseye But Mostly an Eliciting, & Perhaps Illicit, Tea Time

Ash & Emma are sitting on the avocado green grass by the clocktower
Birthmarks exposed   it's a lemon-sorbet day   not that they
really notice   they're bracketed—not in a tangent kind of way   the rest of the
world is the mere tangent

Emma has slackened
She is still effervescent
just lemonade effervescent now
Her mind has been upstaged by her body
by his
smoked eyelids, fluttering bumbling bellies & lost knees
Acutely aware of their movements
of the distance between his body and hers
the lewdly loud space between them feels compressed
          about to burst
Magnetic, esoteric, electric, erotic
                    Rococo or Baroque

She can feel herself expanding in his presence
          growing into her own embedded outlines with power
And somehow,
despite the mint or lemon tinglings in very specific places,
she manages to chew the conversational straw.

Ash is twinned:
     -     one's observing, riding his own high,
thinking to himself how wild it is that he's sober right now,
how attuned they are, how tangible it feels,
and feeling the waves of each other's frequency pulse
as material yet immaterial as the wind or the ocean
capricious, sometimes downright cantankerous,
beyond the rationalising of forecasts or algorithms.
What it is really, is an experience, and a wild one at that—
like a very good batch of space cookies
     -     Meanwhile the other Ash
is enjoying the tango-esque banter,
her strawberry smiles,
and her purple vibrations.

The dial of the clocktower seems to be an ashtray
containing two fun sticks, waiting to be fired up
Although, looking at their ladybird dots
they're definitely flying.

Ash by himself, at a different 4:20
Barefoot & bed marked flashbacks—

A hunch that leads him to a staircase inside the Clock Tower,

up he goes

his fingers following the zigzagging carvings on the wooden handrail

the staircase consists of broken crockery

mottled with dayglow paint

the wall, despite looking crumpled like tin foil,

seems to be made of steel.

Something comes out of Ash's mouth

like belching out glass or having the plastic hiccups

but he makes out the words

he once learnt by rote

« Eh bien ! lui cria-t-elle, n'avais-je pas raison ?

De quoi vous sert votre vitesse ?

Moi, l'emporter ! Et que serait-ce

Si vous portiez une maison ? »

Somehow his mind can see the house on his back,

the rugs, the rocking-chair, tea set, lanterns, dishes, afghans, orchids, as well as the

Devil's ivy, the Spiral Aloe, the high cupboard containing the silver, the crystal, the

Limoges, the Creuset, and the ubiquitous mint,

the layout of his childhood home was there

solid, if slightly granulose, under his index finger.

He keeps on walking up.

Passing by Nora, who is shampooing Mo & Gab, rye drips down to the concrete floor.

He keeps on walking up.

The aseptic & caustic white light of supermarket aisles hurts his eyes,

But he still sees the hares that are racing on the shelves.

He keeps on walking up.

Reaches something that partly resembles a clock,

and a bullseye.

No hands.

He's now in his parents' kitchen,

gridlocked in the dark squares of the wood,

a plate of chicken, pasta and chickpeas with a spicy sauce in front of him.

Gab, Kar, Hab, Rob Nora & Mo are sitting on the grass by the clocktower

Boombox playing *Time Has Come Today*

Anyone knows where Ash & Emma are off to? queries Gab

Exaggerated shrugging & shaking of head

I don't think they've talked about it yet, Nora says with a smile

Too afraid to burst the bubble? Rob asks

*I remember those times…*Hab adds, sharing a rosemary laden look with Rob

Yeah…and knowing Ash, he doesn't know what to do with it. I don't think we've ever seen him like this…so…

In love, Gab completes

Gab and Mo, momentary telepathize.

True, but I was gonna say involved. *He's been pretty laid back about everything the last few years…he's pretty much checked out ever since he quit uni. Boarded up even. Ash has always been good with his hands. He really wanted to be like…a woodworker. Or a carpenter or something like that. But his parents were like 'your grandparents didn't come here for you to become a manual worker.' I guess he felt hemmed in. So he tried, you know. He followed the tracks. Until he felt like it had changed. I guess he felt he wasn't so much on the train as tied to the tracks. He was really flippant about everything…calling everything and everyone 'phony'… He wasn't always wrong…obviously. But he'd gotten so…bitter's not the word. No, he didn't care enough anymore to be bitter. Aloof.*

I cannot imagine what it must be like to calibrate your life to someone else's needs, Kar says. *Maybe I already do, in small ways, but definitely not like that.*

*It's the years wasted trying that make the mind reel…*Gab clarifies, petting the carnations of her choker with her index fingers.

Do you really think you can waste years of your life? Hab plonks on the grass

Perhaps not, Mo replies, *but when things skid out of control and you end up upside-down in a ditch it does feel that way.*

You feel like your life's in a ditch? Gab, surprised

I do ok. Still, it's not what I dreamed for myself.

I don't think many of us here feel that way, Rob points out before adding, *it seems to be tied up with the notion of productivity more than anything…by that I mean, it's the lack of fruition that gives a sense of waste. It's the whole goal-oriented mindset that skews people's sense of time. And we got rid of that.*

I don't know if that's true, Nora contradicts cautiously. She absent-mindedly spins her pendant as she goes on explaining, *I'm not saying I felt the pressure to be or make*

anything, or even that I felt like I was wasting my time. However, I did feel like I had to believe a conclusion that was handed down to me. I felt powerless and aimless because it seemed like the answers were already there, unearthed. Mined for. That all the foraying and figuring out was done for me. Frankly, it felt like I had nowhere to go. And that's exactly what I did, in a roundabout way, I went nowhere to find here.
You did the digging, Rob remarks. *How like us and unlike us.*
How's the exhibition coming along by the way? Kar asks.
Rob & Hab share a look.
Nicely, we just need a few more testimonials with some art to bring it to life. And Mo's installation is totally eye-opening, I can't wait for everyone to see it.

The song ends
silence is the perfect segue
into chirping & buzzing.

The roses that play their ice-cream truck fragrance.
All eyes converge on the dark red roses
climbing up the clock tower.

The dial looms high above everyone and everything.
It beams with a sluggish vanilla or monoi stillness
emulating warmth's ability to freeze frame.

Rob gets two decks of UNO out and starts dealing
7 times 6, the grass is perky, the day frisky.
Heat prints ikat patterns on the horizon, or maybe it's the 4:20.

Framed, Colour Laden & Popping

NIGHT TIME - EMMA IN THE GUEST ROOM OF THE Os - WORM'S EYE
VIEW

Night's ceiling, normally composed of Velcro, has softened into felt

Emma's pop reveries stand out against the dark background

The turquoise lyrics of

Comic Strip flash by

in comic font

Viens petite fille dans mon comic strip

The *Amor Amor* Rose is fuchsia

Viens faire des bulles, viens faire des **WIP**

Des **CLIPS, CRAP,** *des* **BANGS,** *des* **VLOP**

Et des **ZIP, SHEBAM POW, BLOP, WIZZ**

Illustrious fictitional couples

J'distribue les swings et les uppercuts

from Lucy & Ricardo,

Ça fait vlam, ça fait **SPLATCH,** *et ça fait* **CHTUCK**

Maria & Toni,

Ou bien **BOMP,** *ou* **HUMPF,** *parfois même* **PFFF**

Jack & Rose,

ZIP, SHEBAM POW, BLOP, WIZZ

Ross & Rachel,

Viens petite fille dans mon comic strip

Marshall & Lily

Viens faire des bulles, viens faire des **WiP**

Malcolm & Marie

Des **CLiPS, CRAP,** *des* **BANGS,** *des* **VLOP**

frozen in mtv coloured embrace

Et des **ZiP, SHEBAM, POW, BLOP, WiZZ**

Heart jellies **MiAM!**

Viens avec moi par dessus les buildings

E & A in an arrow-pierced heart

Ça fait **WHiN,** *quand on s'envole et puis* **KLiNG**

carved into a cartoon tree

Après quoi je fais **TiLT,** *et ça fait* **BOiNG**

Comic strip projected onto the ceiling:

SHEBAM, POW, BLOP, WiZZ

Frame 1: comic strip versions of Ash & her, standing face to face against a white

background

SHEBAM, POW, BLOP, WiZZ

Frame 2: Closeup of her mellowing & blushing features as she looks at him

Viens petite fille dans mon comic strip

Frame 3: Closeup of his warming & softening features as he looks at her

Viens faire des bulles, viens faire des wip

Frame 4: Wide, both are struck by peach lightning. ZAAAAAAP!

Des clips, crap, *des* bangs, *des* vlop

Frame 5: The jolt has lightened the colours

Et des **ZiP, SHEBAM, POW, BLOP, WiZZ**

LOVE

N'aies pas peur, bébé agrippe-toi **CHRACK**

with the oblong & swooning O

Je suis là **CRASH** *pour te protéger* **TCHLACK**

Dayglow popcorn

Ferme les yeux **CRACK,** *embrasse-moi* **SMACK**

The mint & lemon tinglings

SHEBAM. POW. BLOP. WIZZ

in the form of

SHEBAM. POW. BLOP. WIZZ

tea green & banana yellow sparkles

SHEBAM. POW. BLOP. WIZZ

A randy combination of strums & pedal steel riffs & drums wipe it all away

The summer sizzling & lascivious voice

conjures familiar fingers

…

Hissing onomatopoeias darken

scarlet to crimson

The bramble-lining of night

is crushed into the dark pink hues

of blackberry jam

Kowtow-less Pot & Artichoke Harmony

The Foreign Four and the Coms' crowd are sitting in the last ring of the Pop Pot.

Jam is reffing—*it's freewheeling when it's Jam* Hab warns.

So it is.

The subject is:

> Medical trips and how to cover the costs as a Community.

So far, taking care of one's medical needs has meant leaving the Community to find a pharmacy, a doctor, or a hospital. Some Coms are completely off the grid and therefore have no health insurance. *Less than ideal.*

All the Coms pitch in, dig in,

gathering on the palm of the cupping hand,

pitching picnic tables,

unfurling sundry tablecloths: chequered, chevron, or chintz.

Plates are stacked. Patterns. Crisscrossing black lines on the rim, red rims, frills, flowers, rainbow…Taken, handed, filled.

Pimentaise, grated carrots, roast chicken, chicken subs, taboulet, frites, crudités on toothpicks, fig bread, poppy seed bread, water, lemonade, virgin punch, iced-tea, pineau, cognac, sangria

Anecdotes **chomp, slurp, gulp, clink**

First, we should dig into the profits from our sales. The Community primarily sells oranges and other food stuff as well as some handmade bracelets & earrings. *Then, and that's merely a suggestion, we chip in on a sorta donation or subscription basis for the rest.*

Heads and grunts sandwich in agreement.

The toughest part is gonna be deciding who's in charge of the fund.

Like reffing. In turns.

Right. Right. That makes sense.

How come this issue is only coming up now?

Resources, resources…We only had the one house with the orange trees at first… we've lived hand to mouth for a long time. Building and sowing . And, come to think of it, I don't recall anyone needing urgent care so far. No one's ever come down with anything serious. At least nothing herbs and rest or, as a last resort, a trip to the nearest pharmacy couldn't fix. Come to think of it, I don't think anyone has ever broken a bone here. Sprained, bruised or nicked while doing building work, but nothing worse than that. Or I genuinely don't recall.

So money does circulate here?

Kinda. My parents don't sell stuff, so they don't have any. Not that I know of. But yeah. Anyone is free to go out and sell stuff.

*Not everything though. Not for food. You can't just sell all the fruits and vegetables you produce so it's—*finger air quotes around *"regulated."*

Yeah. The Community first obviously. Otherwise, you're free to have money. But we don't sell stuff within the Community.

The palm is crowded. Subsumed.

The pot is brimming. Without any soapbox or throne stirring.

Discussion groups form around dishes or drinks.

The chicken crowd is relieved. *They*'ve been worried about what to do if the little ones get sick. Lila chimes in. *They* raised their kids just fine, what are *they* so worried about? Booping Seth, who is wrapped around Tom's torso. Anyway, a plan is a good thing to have.

The sangria crowd is in agreement that doing the Pop Pot meetings *this way* is nice once in a while. Upbeat. And *they* get to catch up too. Still, *they*'d never get anything done. But then, *they* got to experiment so why shouldn't the young. In all fairness, can *they* say that the politicians, in their fancy-ass suits, sitting all prim and proper in their semi-circular assemblies, senates, parliament, can *they* say that despite their formal-ass ways *they* get the stuff done? Ha, he got *them* there.

The pimentaise crowd has moved on to homeschooling and have you heard of the Montessori way? Emma mentioned it. It's funny, it's basically *their* way. Formality is buried under a ladleful of taboulet. Mouths are absent-mindedly wiped while opinion & inputs flow freely. Emma, a plate on her lap, on the last ring of the Pop Pot with the other Foreign Four and the young Coms, praises Jam for her out of the box idea. From the Bible to everyone's favourite sitcom, *if there's something we know it's that food unties tongues.*

So that's your reffing style?
Yeah, well, I was never into authority in any form. Not even being it. I tried the conventional way, sitting, and shepherding this—wiggling her fingers as if to draw the words in instead of out— *unbelievably willing flock. Repeating the mantras, the values and going through the list—it just feels contrived. And overbearing. Authoritative. I hate it. I still attend the meetings, and I get where it's coming from, but man, it's creepy. In my opinion.*
I never knew you felt this way too. It is unsettling, you know, the way it feels when we're all repeating the words…I get this weird out of body-like experience. And the unison. It looms over us. I tried to broach the subject with my mum but she said it reminded her of what she loved about church. Like the harmony of singing as one and believing as one. It's not that I find it repellent, like, I get how wonderful it seems on paper or otherwise. For the lonely, the estranged or the misfits. The outsiders—
*You mean the people who created this place—*César cuts in with his pickled interjection.
Jam & Nora sharing a grass-grazing look.
We know where the impulse comes from.
We do. It doesn't change the fact that the put on harmony can feel like taking a bite out of an artichoke.
The silence trails off into gruyère-sticky awkwardness. Stringy.

Breaking bread. And the lucky charm in it says:
Don't Trust Anyone Over Thirty.
One side thinks they know the score. And the other yearns to make their own mark.

Those Desert Sights

The raspberry 8 ushers in the
blueberry 9 which ushers in the
blackcurrant 10.

Everyone is clustered around the bonfire, barring some of the young parents who are
catching up on their sleep. But the rest are here, drinking the Kool-Aid. More or less
figuratively speaking.
No bogarting the tea.
Exulting, reveling around the cactus-like fire.
It's a cropped reality. Or zoomed in. At any rate, a grape not the cluster.
The garishly orange petals of the cactus-like fire flicker. Prodded by the sober breeze.
But the cactus is lithe. Bending, with its ridges, without breaking.
And, somehow, it makes browbeaten jalopy dreams new again.
Mo looks at Hab & Rob,
both sitting, Hab's back resting against Rob's chest,
cheek to cheek, like a Mapplethorpe,
except for the cactus-cast orange glow.
All of a sudden, Mo sees something far down the recesses of his mind,
a silhouette behind a pea-soup screen,
a bright orange light goes on behind the silhouette,
the pea-soup screen is revealed to be a stained-glass window.

Calla Lily

& the silhouette's contours are clearly delineated.

Prickled by the heat

Gab moves back

her eyes saunter along the wave-like outlines of the cactus

topped by a yellow, puckering flower

in the eye of the hubbub yet impervious to it

outlines like grooves around the cactus

like grooves

grooves

grooves

Victrola playing

Gab, clad and coiffed in the flapper style, sings a jazz version of *One Too Many*

Morning

All in black & white

Except for the orange carnations around her wrist

Art deco room, round tables with bouquets of daggers as centre-pieces

slowly blunting & blooming into yellow lilies.

Her voice dances barefoot across the room

while the needle of the victrola slides in the grooves

slides in the grooves

like a blade untethering the sound

like a blade untethering serotonin

in the grooves

the grooves

grooves

Kar wraps her arm around Gab shoulders

Nora is sitting with her parents, Cesar, Nou, Az, Lila, Sid, & Aimée.

Listening as they preface their criticism with tacky & transparent little handles like

'not to be critical but'

Nora and her generation, birds of a beak, the hooked kind.

No such words are used,

but it's Nora

who holds the other side of the generational

can to her ear

& hears what comes through the distorting string.

She looks down at the compass, lying flat in the palm of her hand,

needle points East.

& the pansy looks like an orchid in the orange light.

The eye can see the undulating waves billowing from the flaring petals

heat's frequency

worming its way up

only to be disintegrated by night.

Bouquets or Sprigs of Radio Solstice

The day rises
with a crackling sound,
slightly out of tune,
due to an imbalance
between AMs & PMs
AMs casting their pulpy light over the PMs
& its magnetic seeds aggravate a system already out of whack.

Nora & Emma by the bus.

Butterflies circle the two women. Buzzing with the day's wah wah energy.

Nora: Look at you. Smitten. Can't even keep your mouth from smiling, right?

Emma's giddy grin fizzles.

Emma: I guess so.

Nora: I have to say I didn't see it coming. But, looking at you two, you guys make sense.

Emma: Alright, easy on the love talk.

Emma is wearing her hair down. In tight curls. She has been rollicking in generously straw-blond glory. But the silver in her sky is no moon.

I know everyone thinks I'm a Debbie Downer and I frankly don't care. Yes, it's incredibly fun and pleasurable. Yes it's the cheesy black and white to technicolour miracle that they say it is. I've been in love before, and even though the memory didn't fade it's not quite the same as living it in the moment. Still, I can't lose sight of the fact that this isn't my life and I've got to get back to it.

Nora: You are here. Living. How is this not your life?

Emma: You should know the answer to this better than anyone.

Emma gently grabs the compass resting on Nora's chest.

Most of the butterflies are gone.

only three remain—

arranged like ellipsis.

Mo at & with Luciana & Sara

A slightly crunchy *Sunshine Superman* is playing on the radio.

Mo: How did you guys meet? Were you travelling outside of here? Or did you stumble upon this place?

Sara: I was travelling through a town not too far from here when I spotted Lu, who was selling oranges and was completely absorbed by the trade. I was utterly lovestruck. She was effortlessly elegant without a hint of haughtiness. So, old smitten me bought oranges to get an audience with this fair—

Luciana: Jesus! Sara, come on.

Static pixelates the song.

Sara: She hates compliments.

Luciana: No, I simply find the idea of being pursued disturbing. Yes, you saw me first, BUT, love is consensual. I have to admit I *finger air-quotes around* "recognized" you the minute you entered my eyeline.

Sara: Always challenging my traditional mindset this one. Anyhow, we exchanged letters for a while—

Luciana: And after some light *air-quote* "brainwashing" or "unwashing", she moved here with me.

Mo: No small commitment.

Sara: Well people convert for their partners, and that's what I did. Just not in an *air-quote* "religious" way.

Mo: I mean. It's not that remote from it. It's all ideological.

They don't hear the grumbling & grizzling voice of a distorted Donovan.

Luciana: I sense resistance.

Mo: No, no. I don't even know what you mean by that. No, I'm trying to make sense of it. Embracing one ideology seems like picking Cubism and discarding everything else.

Luciana: We're not talking about aesthetics here, Mo. Cubism doesn't make sense of social issues.

Mo: No, but it's a prism like any ideology. Religious or political.

Luciana: How postmodern of you to claim that collage is the superior way to see the world.

Gushing static fills the room with black & white confetti.

They're choosing to ignore it.

Ash & Gab sitting at one of the round tables. Lemongrass bouquet at the centre.

Weeks of lemon or grapefruit sun have altered the acidity level of the sky.

Something's a-coming.

Ash is sitting straight. Hands on his lap.

Gab, forearms against the table, mic feedback free, carnations on her right wrist, twists Ash's crank.

Gab: We haven't talked much since we got here.

Ash: Well, frankly? I just thought you were avoiding me or something.

For the first time in years, his wheel is spinning.

Ash's leg starts jerking. Buzzing.

Gab: Why is that?

He shrugs. Noise of tv static.

About Emma—

Ash: I don't know. I don't know if it's because of me or not, but you've barely said a word to her since we got here.

Gab: Oh man…it's so not about you.

Ash: I don't know I'm just…

The paisley patterns of his red bandana are buzzing

Gab: Ash, we said we didn't love each other that way. I don't know about you, but I sure meant it. Alright? I have nothing against Emma. We're just not on the same, like, wavelength.

Ash: Ok, ok. Sorry. I just don't get it cause you are both…I don't know…you exude something similar.

Gab: I really don't know what to make of that.

The air is conducive. Wireless.

Ash: Frankly, in a good and in a bad way. Like, there is this energy around you, like static, like restlessness and, probably stress. But there's also those waves. Man, this is gonna sound way out there but like your inner worlds, there's so much light and darkness and colour coming from you. You just come across as interesting people. Hurdy gurdy buzz.

Gab: Like Nora isn't interesting. Or Mo for that matter.

Ash: Yeah, no they are. But they are so composed and contained. It's all inside and not in a mysterious way.

Gab: Dude, you just dig tortured chicks.

His eyeline drops down to her bracelet and bounces back up.

Ash: It was so moving to hear you sing again. I meant to tell you. You cast a spell there. I guess that's what I mean. Mo & Nora are clearcut leaders. There's nothing fuzzy about it. You're not. You seem like a loner. Just like Emma. And yet, there's something magnetic about you two.

Gab: Ash, you just like our vibe. Don't project more than what it actually is.

She brings her plait over her shoulder,

a chocolate ear of wheat,

at least that's how it looks to Ash.

Ash & Emma sit down in the shadow of the clock tower.

The roses' fragrance, dayglow pink, curlicues around them.

The breeze plucks the tight thin strings of electricity of the neck of this long summer's day.

It produces an ethereal sound.

Daisies in their hair, ladybirds on their limbs, ginger on their breath & exuding post-making it mellowness & birthmarks showing.

Emma: You know, Nora told me we're welcome to stay here if we want to.

Ash: For real? I had no idea. I was kinda hoping they would offer though.

Emma: I know right! It's like this place where you don't have to buy time, I mean you still have to participate in the teeny society, but it's less demanding. You can just *be*.

Ash: It's less phony too because of that. Cause you don't have to pretend to care about shit you don't care about. It's not a fucking competition. As if anyone could win at capitalism.

Emma: That's it. Although it's not like this life doesn't have a downside too. But, I mean, I dunno, it seems so freaking manageable by comparison. And anyway, it doesn't have to be forever. I don't know that I'd like to stay put forever. But just to know that this place exists. Like a time out. An actual freaking vacation.

Ash: I hear ya. So, we'll see each other.

Emma: Er…I mean I kind of assumed that…yeah?

Ash: Yeah!

The music roly-polies around them

while

Ash plaits a sprig of rye into her hair

& into a crown

clouded with yarrow.

& the ladybird bumps are mostly gone.

Gab & Kar, by the train tracks, wild oats all around.

Gab, ikat maxi dress, lying down on an afghan. Kar, in a wrap dress striped with lines of inverted green & red triangles, sitting cross-legged & weaving a raffia basket.

A patch of tall grass chirps.

Gab: Come to think of it, maybe, on some level, I chose waitressing for this purpose. It's a big *maybe* though. But, wouldn't it be nice, you know? Getting yourself where you need to be, or ish, without thinking about it?

Gab's gaze drops down from a couple of oddly shaped clouds against a blue backdrop to Kar.

Kar acquiesces, head bow down, sharply focused. As sharp as the tips of her inverted triangles.

The other night got me looking back. I've been replaying the last few years in my head. Wondering why I didn't try before.

Kar: You said everyone had been telling you it's hopeless. '*A pipe dream*' whatever that means.

Gab smiles at the pipe shaped cumulus on the azure canvas. *Ceci n'est pas une pipe.* No, it isn't.

Gab: Yeah, but it shouldn't have kept me from trying. Or just singing for myself. I didn't allow myself to sing cause I didn't think it would bring me fame…that's screwed up.

Kar: I'm just saying what you told me.

Still not looking up. Weaving.

Gab sits up, leaning back on her hands.

Gab: Kar, what's wrong?

Kar still doesn't look up. Just shrugs. Her arms & legs slashed by the needle-like tip of the triangles.

Gab: I know this move too well (with a coaxing smile). Please tell me.

Kar drops everything and finally looks up.

Kar: It's not against you. I mean a little, but I know it's dumb.

Their voices suddenly seem coated with a sci-fi eeriness

Gab: Kar...

as if trapped between two antennas

like soaring signals spiked by the day's vibrancy.

Kar: I genuinely don't get why you're so stoked about going back cause everything you've said...You hate it there. And, and, I'm sad. Nora's the only one who's ever left me and it really, really hurt. She's always been like my sister. And you. You just do the same.

Gab: I've asked you to come, and you haven't mentioned it. Not even once. Have you even like, given it a think?

Kar: My parents would take it the wrong way.

Gab: Come on!

Kar: They built this place for us. For us to have what they didn't. How does it look if I just thumb my nose at them?

A dragonfly appears from beyond the train tracks and hovers over them. It siphons the interfering signals stowed away in the smallest units of their conversations. Casting down, in return, the mitigating scent of mint paired with rosemary.

Gab: Kar, they built their Shangri-La based on their dreams and hopes. Based on needs created by the life they lived out there. Yeah they want to protect you but honestly I'm sure you'd appreciate it a lot more if you knew what it's responding to. And they'd appreciate you knowing the difference between blindly agreeing and being convinced. Also, they probably didn't build this place for it to become a grateful-slash-guilt prison for their children. At least, I hope they didn't.

Kar: It's really gone over your head, hasn't it? This isn't a place, it's a group of people. It's a community. It's not just about moving geographically; it's about leaving people.

Gab: Ok, but you gotta do what's right for you. Nora understands it, yet she did what she had to to be happy. Is she the only one who's broken away from the group?

Kar: Za, one of the founders, actually the guy who came up with the idea to dig the Pop Pot and he left about 10 years ago. Had to take care of his dying mother. I think he was supposed to come back but never did. Never even heard from him since. And Sara left once.

Gab: I'm not surprised.

Kar: But she came back.

Gab: Yeah. Kar, cause it doesn't have to be for good.

The breeze pipes down & the evening scrapes the sci-fi coating off their voices. The dragonfly finally flies away.

If you don't wanna come then don't, but don't turn down an opportunity cause you're afraid of what others might think. I mean, isn't what the Community tried to move away from in the first place?

Kar: I just don't know if I have the bandwidth…

Gab MUAHS Kar's cheek.

Gab: I've got you, babe. And this place, and its people, is still going to be here for you.

The triangles convex into circles

which split into concentric circles

the inner one full, ripe,

the outside one light green with a black outline,

almost like a pupil in an iris.

Kar slides her hand up a sprig of wild oats, leaving the sprig seedless before scattering the content of her palm.

The acid AMs are not done expanding

infringing

on the dark berry PMs.

Sparkling seeds bump in the night

and their crude light scars the night.

A Shapeshifting Ballad of Figuration (part 1) Composed or Complained by Coattail Riders for Reluctant Undertakers

It's the day of the exhibit. The tallest pulp-filled glass of a day.

Everyone gathers in a mosquito-repellent & motley cloud of scents. From cloves, mint, citronella to lemongrass.

All huddled in volkswagen-van spirit & about to listen & read the highlighted quotes of the Community's iconographic geography.

Only today the quotes' syntax and symbolism are propped up in a ballad of acoustic interpretation. Where ambiguity sets the ambiance of ambivalence.

The background music consists of mosquitoes, bees, bumblebees, & wasps playing the hurdy gurdy while the blackbirds, magpies, robins, & goldfinches blow the brass to the unresponsive wind.

On their way to the bus, the site of the first exhibit, Nora draws her peers' attention to the gathering tables

suddenly hypnotically spinning.

Suspenseful & *Vertigo*-esque,

albeit with the eye-duping & mind-loosening potency of illusion.

Only the Fur of Further & Undertaker Digs

Hab & Rob lead the file of Coms into the dark bus. Spayed windows & shrouded windshield. Seats like 80s-clad tombstones lit from below. Tokens of the past lying like flowers or offerings. The white gurney light lodges itself in the creases of the founders' faces. Some are on the cozy side of narrow. Others are on the lung-crushing & clammy hands side. Same bus. Everyone turns around. Hab turns on the projector screwed onto the ceiling. The irksome buzz of flies—number unknown—distracts some. Most. A moving landscape appears on the shrouded windshield. Kaleidoscopic lights are also cast onto the Merry Prankster ceiling. Hands swat the bugs away. The sinister graveyard stiffness is stretched & mellowed by movement into liveliness. There's a sound of engine purring. & the buzzing of the flies, like a glitch. Drawing everyone's attention away from the seat & the fossilised bones of a never-visited past.

Reactions range from perplexed, mildly amused, rankled to dampened. Lila, Abe, and Mal, all claustrophobic, all wan. César, arms flailing, already venting. This bus means a lot to him. How dare they? Az, a hand on César's shoulder, shoulders César's rant. Brace yourself man, this is only the first stop. I'm done, Az. I just can't stand there and let them skewer the most beautiful things in my life without fully losing it. I can't take it. Cés, it's not about taking anything. It's about listening. Emerald-eyed Gloria tousles the forever-young-to-her Cés out of his griping. Mig, frosted-tips & baby-smooth-faced when he joined the Community with his partner Mel, now Juanez-haired & goatee, can't believe he's never been on the bus before. Mel, fuller eyebrows & now garçonne haircut, chuckles. She's reminded of their meet-cute at a football game, where she rescued his defenseless wallet in the middle of a packed stadium. School's in session, then.

Musings Bordering on Museum & Margin-mongering Editorial Commentary
They arrive at the Pop Pot. Some kind of tarpaulin tops off to the sheltering wood
panels of the last and highest ring keeping the light out. Closed fist. Or tuna can. Lila
rushes out. Feeling a smothering hand on her face. The nagging buzz of bugs, flies,
wasps and mosquitoes, smudges the writing like sweaty fingers. Spotlights from the
last ring reveal, or rather emphasize, the palm. Plaited tapestry wall hangings rolled
up and placed on the floor to form the peace sign with a red pail where the reffing
stool usually is. Emma & polka-dot-wearing Mei & Al & Silvia are contemplating the
pretty paisley spoons they've found beside the pail. The chest of instruments is
nowhere to be found. The place looks like an art gallery humming *If you're going to
San Francisco* & dancing in the incandescent light of incense sticks. It all seems to
hark back to the good ole Pentagon Levitating or Exorcising days. All mined down to
the paisley bedrock. Newspaper flowers sprout headlines from the 60s to the late 80s.
The revolutions of the Iberian Peninsula or the final pages of the drawn-out Cold
War. Buzzzzz. Clay mushrooms with removable caps quote famous activists &
Community founders. *It's not about digging your way out of reality but digging your
hole in it.* The latter's names are found on decorated shovels. Lying flat on the
benches. Benchmarks. No soundbites, no scoring, no ambiance setting noises.
Nothing but their reactions, trapped in by the lid. & the bugs. The place at once smells
like fresh lemons & lemon scented dish soap. A handful of strategically placed
mirrors, leaning against the profane pews, on the second ring, reflect, or rather echo
the reality in the Pop Pot as well as the reflected realities. Ash peers into one from one
vantage point. Then another. Then another. Cards with the founders as the Ace of
Spades next to face-down & orange-tree-in-art-nouveau-style-motif tarot cards.
Emma flips one of the cards. Blank. Ash & Gab & Mo are reminded of their private
joke. Ela fingers the cards, bringing her hand to her chest, up to the V at the base of
the throat, fumbling for something that's missing. Catching Emma & Kar's attention
with her lasso-like birthmark.
Most of the installation consists of superimposed elements. Embedded or juxtaposed.
All encapsulated. It doesn't seem to be the proselytising kind of prose, but it does
swing the fringes of the mind.

Nora praises the work of the two young men. Jam chimes in. Stoked. She digs the
mirrors & the mushrooms. Abe, like someone who got his head stuck in a plastic bag,
asks how they managed to get the tarp up and is it all going to be like this cause he's

wrecked. Heavy looks from Lila & Mal speak volumes. Lu finds it all inspired and *air-quotes* "shrewdly irreverent" without being able to explain how so. Sara complains about the lingering smell of dish soap. Pungent. Although others interject, they could barely smell it. Or they love it anyway. Less pushback. Can we get those Ace of Spades cards? Rob & Hab are not fielding questions until the end of the field trip. César remains unimpressed by what the fishbowl blues implies.

Pins and Needles Struck by the Skull Sipping Peacock Feather Wearer

And they walk through the space that's become an enigma to the next riddle. The clock tower. On the stones, behind and above the roses, organs, disconnected from each other by broken art nouveau style ties, dark with decay. Rotten organs transplanted onto the clock tower. Stickers. At the centre of the heart, time's hands, bleeding. The rest of it is overtaken by the sporous black of rot. The clock tower, now transfigured into an aged pothead. The roses, their youthful outward appearance. Grateful. Yet Dead. All of it conjures the headstone-seats, clattering teeth, chrysanthemums. Only one way to be underground and keep Time at bay. Still requires shovels. The undertaking kind.

Toni, Rob's brother, after taking a drag on his ciggie and blowing the smoke out, goes, *all of this is bumming me out. Why you gotta be so glum?* Donna, their sister, walks over to Rob and loops her arm around his. Gab & Ash are searching for, and telepathically beckoning, Mo's gaze. But he's staring at the dark heart. Nora sidles next to him. *That's your idea right? It's that obvious?* He looks around to see if anyone else has registered:

They roped you in, they might as well put your credentials to use.

The claustrophobic 3 have rallied. Off the cuff reviews are traded. Others thumb through the already read pages. While the buzz of the acoustic ballad continues in the background.

Flipping the Furrowed Frame on the Railed Against Forerunners (Riveted Coattail Riders)

>The goodbye portion of the tracks is framed with what looks like a funeral wreath. Not far from it, tree roots have been Frankenstein transplanted to the tracks. Not actual tree roots though. A painted wooden panel was grafted onto the tracks. Rob & Mo, who've run off without a word, come back with bags of rosemary crowns & thyme cuffs for everyone. Hab invites the founders to, one by one, identify their goodbye & share a story about the person, or people, it is addressed to. Nora joins Kar & Jam to listen. And so do the families, like Rob's parents, who arrived later on. Soon the entire 2nd generation of Coms is sitting down, looking up at their elders in the same avid & reverent way that sunflowers look up to the sun. So do the Foreign Four. While the founders relish in an exercise that they'd assumed would turn to earsplitting vinegar, but instead is merely acidly perfumed & flavoured like citrus. The limelight is theirs.<

Freeform Peeling

They walk on, boundlessly chatting. Sketching skewed portraits of family dynamics. Of gatekeepers of truth. To conclude that it's simply the entitlement that comes with experience. At last. Ironic for a gateless & fenceless community. Emma watches, Ash is distracted by the ducktail on the back of Hab's head. She tries to get a hold of his hand, but Ash encases them in the pockets of his jeans.

They finally arrive at the House. The one with sanguine beams & shutters & a curled hand on its front door. Only, the elements & neglect have taken their toll. The healthy red has dulled & sagged while the white façade has wrinkled and blotched.

Hab asks Ela to come forward to lead them in. On the door, the hand, now corroded, remains untouched.

The shutters are shut. Like a clenched jaw. With gritted teeth. Only slivers of lights are able make their way in and they land on the opposite wall. Looking traced. Artificial. Or like scrubbed up neon lights. The buzz ballad fades out, signaling an end or transition of some form.

A Morphing Ballad of Figuration (part 2)
Kitchen Sink Magic & A Lack of Vitamin C Flare Up
'n' Deference

INT: IN THE HOUSE

Not-Solely-Performative Clean-in & Combustible Wallpaper & Outburst Prompt
Sink

Rob flicks the switch releasing an unkind phosphorescent light. The kind that brings the stale smell of illness to your nostrils. Even though everything is the same. Same staggered row of copper pots that look like exclamation marks on a sugar white wall, same wicker elephant side table, same newspaper rack, same cream sofa clad with a patchwork afghan, same delicate crochet flowers run like lily pads floating on the coffee table. The same lime snowflakes on the same potpourris.

Yet,

the dust glazing gives it a morbid pallor.

Ela's pansy hair wilts.

Rob guides them to the dark kitchen, where the shutters are also shut & the phosphorescent light takes away the *vint* of vintage, and where buckets & bowls & basins & sponges & soaps await for them on the Formica table with brooms & mops resting on one side.

SAL, *knee jerk reaction*: **Are you having a laugh?**

ELA, *with the sharp, brief sting of a needle*: **It's time we took care of this house, Sal.**

They confer. Tasks are assigned. Ela wants the kitchen to herself. Alright.

Gab, who is in charge of the entertainment room with Yann & Nou, comes back to the kitchen to empty their bucket.

GAB: This is gonna sound like a dumb question but, who's house is it?

ELA: No one's. Not anymore. We all lived here at first. Then we decided it'd be safer, for the harmony of the Community, if we all had individual homes. Sal & Silvia lived here too when they first arrived here. But then, they moved out and it was meant to be for Hamza and his family when he came back with them. Which, as you know, never happened.

Ela doesn't look at Gab who gets a sense that this is a hole that hasn't been plugged. An amphitheatre-sized hole. So she takes the bucket Ela has kindly refilled for her and gets back to her task.

Whistle while you work is hummed, sung, and, obviously, whistled.

Emma & Ash & Mo, in charge of bathrooms & bedrooms, notice that the mirrors are showing double.

Abe, who is in charge of one of the bathrooms, comes back with his bowl. Plonks it on the corrugated side of the sink, and sits at the Formica table.

ABE: Do you mind giving it a rinse for me, love? I'm beat. All this shut-in business is sapping…

ELA, *holding her circled elbow in her hand, turns around and vents*: **I don't have the bandwidth for this right now, ok? Can't you see that I'm upset?**

She catches her reflection in the not-so-benign stainless steel. Or someone else's reflection. A cruel funhouse mirror reflection.

ABE: Alright, alright. Sorry. Geez. What's wrong?

The kitchen cabinets all turn the same shade of orange

the kind that's almost white with a blue crux

the votive candle kind.

ELA: Geez? What's wrong? So self-absorbed you can't even see…

ABE: Now you're not being fair.

The lemon trees of wallpaper ignite the roots up the leaves & fruit.

ELA: Fuck fair, Abe! This is the house I found for us. For our Community. And look at the state of it. All because Za left. _I_ found this house. _I_ organised the move. But for some god forsaken reason it became all about Za. The big shot Weatherman-style radical. "He stuck it to the colonisers." And little me, the mere primary school teacher. Who cares that I left my struggling parents, and worst of all, my loving mother to make my life what I thought it should be. Sacrificed my mama for this. Well fuck that. I loved Za, but this was my doing and I was erased. I left my family, my mother behind...

Abe stands up and hugs his weeping wife.

The room settles down.

The walls have ears.

ELA: I stuck by this Community at the expense of my family. Za chose his family and yet we've been pining for him.

ABE: I know. I'm sorry, love.

Nora, who's been eavesdropping from the living-room, comes in and joins the hug.

Nora's gaze is briefly drawn to the coil burners.

NORA: You know, I'm sure they'd be happy to see you guys. Even after all this time.

ELA: I don't know, cielo, it would probably be excruciatingly painful. It's not cured yet.

The hug loosens.

Ela looks down at the compass on her daughter's chest.

NORA: Mama, you can't heal something that's neglected.

ABE: I'd say it's more akin to a peeled orange. You're never going to get it back the way it was. But, hey, it doesn't mean you can't do nothing good with it.

ELA, *giving Abe a kiss*: **Mi media naranja.**

A palliative not a panacea.

Brooms, pails, sponges, basins, and soaps are returned to the kitchen.

Shutters unclench & fold open.

The evening washes the house with a blend mint & jasmine light.

Ellipsis

EXT: IN THE GARDEN

Harp Strumming Flowers 'n' Pictures & An Unpacked Pachyderm & Homespun Yoyos

Mo & Ash lose their train of thought looking at the flashback inducing bougainvillea.

Flashback

of a young Mo contemplating the wallpaper of his mother's study as she worked on her lectures.

Flashback

of Vovo using her trellis of roses to illustrate the trajectory of immigrant families through the generations. 'The only way is up.'

Mo is first to snap out of it. He pats his friend on the shoulder. They finally join the rest of the group.

Mo's photographs are there, at the feet of the first row of orange trees. In floating frames. Black and white. Herbs as well as dry flowers & citrus fruit wedges add colour and texture. Although the pictures in themselves don't add much to what's been said. They're an eyeful of the same arguments. Simply easier to survey.

The farewell carved tracks & rosemary & yarrows & geraniums & the Os living-room & mint & pansies & orange slices & the clock tower & lemon wedges & thyme & lavender & the Pop Pot & a round slice of grapefruit & violas & the bus & lemon & lime pulp & a motley crew of petal & herbs & paisley ribbons

A Kente clad Jam wraps her arms around her parents' shoulders,

yarns, invisible to the naked eye, wrapped around their hands. Natural yarn spinners.

CÉSAR: Alright. Since we're wrapping things up, you boys might as well reveal the deep message behind today's fuss.

YAS: Cés, come on.

CÉSAR: No, Yas, I'm dead serious. We've been humouring you two all day, now I'd like you to have the guts to tell me what you think is wrong with the place that we've built with the sweat of our brow & back.

Cut to the living-room, the elephant side table shakes the cobwebs off its tusks.

NORA, *weighs in before Hab & Rob get a word in:* You can't take it personally, Cés. It's not a put down. It's not like that. We all get that you've built this place. It's your ideal. But we end up trapped in your ideal. In someone else's Utopia. And that's what some of you can't wrap your heads around. Someone else's Utopia is just like everywhere or nowhere. Not yours to shape or claim. We're somehow stuck in the middle with you & sidelined.

CÉSAR: Poor you. Wanna ask your friends how much worse they've had it?

AZ: Cés, come on, man. We've been there. Stop being so defensive.

CÉSAR: No, I'm not... I'm... I'm sick and tired of the ungratefulness.

Silence where one could easily insert a stirring if mushy song to underscore the emotional load of the moment. All recognise it. Particularly the parents who have been on both sides of this ballad of dissatisfaction. Ash cast a hooded glance at the bougainvillea.

Ela walks up to César, left of Nora,

then embraces César.

A fazed César breaks down.

Reeled in by Ela.

ELA: Be kind. Be compassionate.

Progress is like a folk song. Passed down. Sometimes, lay down. But never quite pinned down.

KAR, *chimes in*: like I told Gab—it's not about the place it's about the people. We keep circling it but let's be clear—the relationships here are what matters. The rest is malleable. Replaceable even. Our bond, we can take it anywhere. We just need to work on it.

YANN*'s soft worded rebuttal*: I don't think you're too right about that. Geography is not something you just slide into and out of without it affecting you. But I guess, you have nothing to compare this too. That's on us. But I'm sure these guys can back me up on this.

The entire Community is clustered in the garden, by the orange trees. The fruit that allowed them to push the walls of the Community. The fruit that brought Luciana & Sara together. Currency. Current.

The juice which could electrify the entire Community. If they ever got sick of their acoustic lifestyle.

The Coms power on, through the operatic amplitude of the day. The bugs resume their summertime buzz while conversations crisscross the garden. In the end, all agree that there is only one way to manage the constant tug of war between the knowledge gleaned through experience & the knowledge that comes from the intuition of inexperience; communication. Without the drone of pent up buggings or the proliferating & pissing-in-the-wind buzzwords. To restore balance. Otherwise experience is stuck on the heavy side of the seesaw.

Ellipsis

Closing With a Saffron 'n' Turmeric Accompaniment

Togetherness in the form of four-legged pieces of furniture are brought to the garden. Paellas, plural for plurality of tastes, are served under a cerulean sky & citronella candles are lit.

Most of the meal is consumed with coca cola music from *Livin' on a Prayer*, *A Minha Casinha*, *Tainted Love*, *L'aventurier*, *Take On Me*, *Marcia Baïla*, *A Town Called Malice*, *Let's Dance*, *Fiesta en América*, *Like a Prayer*. Not the best pairing, yet still enjoyable.

However, as the discussion of dessert arises, Hab & Rob slips out to turn the music off and bring over the instrument chest. Sara rushes out and comes back with her guitar. Az, Mal, Sal & Tom each grab an instrument. Respectively tambourine, harmonica, djembe & castanets. Gab joins them as they set up. Facing the house & guests. The trees as their backdrop.

They first perform *The Times They Are A-Changin'*

& some welcome it as a homage

while others feel betrayed by the last verse's lack of generational loyalty & how it seems to conspire with youth against them.

My Back Pages follows

& they don't know if it's a coke & paella pairing situation or if their sticky puzzlement isn't the result of coke being thrown at them.

Jam & Kar & Rob join her for the finale: *The Circle Game*.

Humanity can come together on one side of the seesaw, but still, it won't outweigh Time.

As the elastic solar time comes to the limit of its expandable power, they unanimously resolve to earmark this day in future calendar: the (Coalition-Building) Solstice Festival of Arts & History.
All leave. Apart from the Foreign Four & Nora & Kar & Rob & Hab who decide to sleep in the house.

Prior: Lifting the Mushroom Cap to Find Baked In & Rambling Narrators & Narratives

We walk back the timeline
to the train tracks tales
for a two-finger tap focus
on cloud-contained reminiscence.

On the way back from the train tracks, Emma, white bardot top & saffron muslin shorts, birthmark exposed, replays Lila & Sid's tale of growing social awareness. Rejected. Rebuffed. Rebuked. Sid, showcasing his accordion skills with cadence & elegance, did the bulk of the horizontal work while Lila's tasks were vertical ones. Like the vertical stripes of her outfit. Informing, galvanizing, & uplifting. Sid's detour-taking narrative style—*that reminds me of something you kids missed out on, the good 'ole hitchhiking days*—in contrast to Lila's, whose interventions were pithy, straight-lined. Her voice walked steadfastly from point A to B to C etc…from one conjunction or connectors or another. Whereas Sid, the performer, played with the whole range of emotivity from rhythm, tone to emoting.

/

An empty sofa / older Ted Mosby's voice: *Kids* / Emma's parents on the sofa / how did she get here from thinking about Lila & Sid's story? / one free space on the sofa / spare the rod but take away the remote / sitcom time / was it the comment about having just the right number of chairs for a meeting? / one free space / older Ted Mosby's voice: *Kids this is the story of* / Lila's voice *Too many chairs and it looks like people didn't show up* / she can't fill the free space / she's not allowed to / Lila's voice *not enough chair and you end up with a standing meeting because you don't want anyone to feel left out* / split in three / they're ignoring her & laughing at the TV / seat cushions / their indifference equals a cartoon anvil squashing her to death / older Ted Mosby's voice: *Kids, love is not a given thing. You may feel you're owed love. Especially when you're giving it. But don't be mistaken. Even the love that swaddles us and nourishes us can be reneged. And you'll not only need to wean, but you'll need to learn to provide for yourself* / brown leather sofa that used to leave brown scales on her hands / the sofa's gone & white walls hem her in / older Ted Mosby's voice: *Kids, everyone has to overcome their share of obstacles in life. They're the result of circumstances out of our control. But you'll find that the most challenging obstacles are the ones we set up for ourselves* / with this Emma is taken back to a flurry of moments / less moments than seats she herself refused to fill / rooms she avoided / excuse-slips she wished she could rescind / Ally McBeal's voice: *I look at the pictures on the walls, pictures of moments I didn't miss and I feel, this, this wave of nostalgic happiness washing over me. It makes me wonder why every so often I keep myself from being happy* / the irony of these voices / voices that evoke friends & social settings / Lila's voice *then you have the people who I'm certain believed in the cause and still couldn't bring themselves to come to the meetings. They required another kind of arm-twisting. The hand-holding kind* / by herself in her white-walled apartment / eating with her favourite spoon / older Ted Mosby's voice: *Now kids, this was no ordinary spoon, it was one of few things she had been able to hold on to that reminded her of her childhood. Before she left in a blaze of, well, not glory. And for a while, it was her only piece of cutlery. But even now that she has more than this stolen coffee spoon, she still eats with it every single day* / Ally McBeal's voice: *Yes, I eat with it every single day. Some people might say it's peculiar, odd or even quirky, and, if I'm being honest, I don't really mind or care. I like being peculiar, odd, quirky. And I like my spoon. I find it comforting. Feeling the pretty curlicues on the handle with my fingertips. I love how it breaks my food into perfectly bitesize mouthfuls. It keeps me from scarfing down the one actual meal a day I can afford. See, it's more than just a quirk. It's a mindset.*

Heya is Kar's greeting as she hoops her arm around Emma's. Gab, who's hooped to Kar's other arm, smiles a toothless, lip-padded smile.

On the way back from the train tracks, Ash, minus a soaked through red bandana, tucked in his pocket, birthmark exposed, reflects on César words: *drifting and bumming. Not literally obviously, what I mean is: well, I had checked out. Someone pointed me in a direction and shuffled there. I tell you, I was mighty unmotivated and that's why I could never hold down a job. My parents were oh so patient...ahhhh... mighty patient.*

/

A voice with fringes & a tipped cowboy hat: *somewhere in the west there was a guy. A guy I wanna tell ya about. Goes by Ash & he's always got his head wrapped in some bandana* / César's voice: *they did everything so that I'd sort myself out. They gave it to me straight 'you can't go on like this son. You're going nowhere. Pick a row and ho it, son. It's that simple. Pick a row* / shelves in a fridge / the back of someone's head with the upside down paisley triangle of a bandana / imagined Holden Caulfield voice: *alright if you really want to know well then I should probably tell you the whole thing from the beginning. From my lousy childhood with my parents on my case from the start* / Ash's mum crouching in front of the fridge. Sorting out the shelves / *they wanted me to take after them and be a binder. My father was an accountant, that should tell you plenty about him, and my mother, my mother. She was a stay-at-home mother and man did she work at that home. Every morning she'd organise the first shelf with what was going to be eaten that day and move up the stuff from the rest of the shelves. Some morning ritual she took on before I was even born. Anyway, they weren't too bad, they cared, they cared so damn much. They wanted for me to have everything, even if they had to shove it down my throat. Like tennis. Boy, that's one boring-ass sport and I told them so, but they made me do it anyway which made me wonder what it was all about. Now I know. Just plain old phony-ass ideas. Anyway, I'm hard on them, I'm aware of that. But you know, 'good intentions' and all that. They weren't all that bad. I liked them fine when they relaxed. I liked them when we were at the pond, feeding slash I guess killing the ducks* / yellow pedal boats & picnic tables & ice cream truck & swans & ducks / *they were so damn uptight the rest of the time it was cool to see them goof off* / Ash's mum dark hair tied up by a black scrunchie into a low ponytail & Ash's dad wearing one of the Hawaiian shirts reserved for such occasions / *they really weren't that bad honestly. It's the looking over my shoulder that drove me mad. I've chipped away at it, at their gaze, but I tell you it's there, lodged in my shoulder. Anyway, it all went south when I went to college. Boy, they were proud at first. Prancing like damn peacocks. They made it such a phony fucking big deal. Their son: the engineer. But then the studies got hard.*

138

I started doing not so well… 'just do the work. Buckle down and do it.' Like I was twiddling my thumb or jerking off instead. So I just flunked out. They were foaming at the mouth but by that point I had stopped giving a flying fuck. Yeah, they won't talk to me anymore, but I don't give a flying fuck. Can't keep eating the bread that's going to kill you from the inside out. You just can't / fringed & cowboy-hatted voice: *That's Ash for ya. Not a bad fella. Part rolling stone, part tramp. Yeah, that about wraps things up. You see where he's at now, not doing too bad for himself. At a crossroad. But then again, most of them are. Anyways, see you down the road.*
Ash looks around. Clocks Emma with Gab & Kar. Spots Abe, who's smiling right at him.

On the way back from the train tracks, Mo walks along with Hab & Rob while his mind peruses Omar's monologue. *Remember how much I used to hate this place? I felt out of my mind with my rage when we moved here. I was a broken record of 'I hate you for taking me away from my friends. I hate this place. I don't want to live like old people in the olden days.' Everything about this place set me reeling with a rabid rage… and especially the wallpaper in the house. I swear, it was physical; like screaming my head off and bashing shit. Remember mum? How I'd lock myself up in the 80s room of the house playing with the pinball machine and listening to records. I reckon it's the only place where I didn't feel like I would die from the overwhelming rage inside. It took me a long long, long time to get over it. If it wasn't for that pinball machine… for that room.*

/

Mo / facing us / sitting on a bed / 1940s camp blanket / walls plastered with posters behind him / bands like Simple Minds, Cabaret Voltaire / he's wearing white crew-neck t-shirt / a black & cream vest / grey suit pants / his unakite bracelet on his left wrist / he's looking right at us saying:
Ferris Bueller's voice: *This isn't my room. Neither of my rooms in fact. Because yeah, my parents got divorced when I was 7 because as it turns out my dad was not the love of my mum's life. Bummer. Anyway, the result for me is: two rooms. Neither of them looks like this. But my rooms aren't really what I want to talk about.*
Mo—still wearing the same outfit—in front of his mother's house / 3 storeys / attached / white façade / Brown shutters / same outfit / in Ferris Bueller's voice: *mum got the house and primary custody. So this is my home five days out of seven.* Opens the door and walks in / Porcelain elephant by the door. Keys on its back / the hall

leads right into the sitting-room with a spiral staircase / damask wallpaper everywhere / Ferris Bueller's voice: *Dig this* he says and sits in the suede, emerald-coloured sofa & puts his feet on the coffee table by the tray with the moroccan tea set / hands behind his head Ferris Bueller's voice: *pretty sweet, right? Mum doesn't make tons as a college professor but she sure knows how to spend it.*

Mo—still wearing the same outfit— in front of a shabby looking door / number 13 / in a building / opens the door / slightly distorted Ferris Bueller voice: *now my dad hasn't been doing so swell.* Side table by the door with a tiny wooden elephant & a framed portrait of Mo minus front teeth & a lantern. A wooden Hamsa hangs on the wall opposite the front door. *He used to be a team-manager in the phone company he works for, but unfortunately he got demoted due to budget cuts. That plus my mum dumping him for another man…Well let's just say the man's been down since then* / striped wallpaper: brown, green, yellow / and apple-green wallpaper in the bedroom / goes through the threadbare kitchen into the sitting-room / cream-colour sofa / 2 seats / a bulbous TV mounted on a flaxen piece of furniture / a coffee-but-really-everything table / and foosball table next to the corridor that leads to the other rooms of the apartment / Mo stands between the sofa and the coffee-but-really-everything table / spinning his unakite bracelet around his left wrist / in Veronica Mars' voice: *I mean it's nice. It's just a little sad. Like a deflated balloon or tv without cable. I love my dad, but I have to admit that I didn't exactly look forward to the weekends here with him down in the dumps. I know it's a cold heartless thing to say. I tried to cheer him up, but nothing made a dent in his gloominess. He wallowed in it. Sometimes he'd cry himself to sleep at night. It was like he was next to me because the partition wall between our two rooms was incredibly thin. My mum on the other hand, well she handled her emotions very differently. She wrote it down or drew it away and it would end up boxed up in her office. I take after her that way. But then, I don't think either of us, Mum and I, we've ever known heartbreak.*

Ash squeezes Mo's shoulder.

On the way back from the train tracks, Gab, arms locked with Kar's, finds herself stuck going over Az's story. *I think it was 2010. Or was it 2012? No, it definitely was a world cup year. Oh yes I remember. It was in 2010. South Africa year.* Az famously went back on the grid to stay with his sister and babysit/follow the games. Az could live without following the league matches and any other sport but not the Euro Cup or the World Cup. *Anyway, I ran into a friend from school. Someone I hadn't seen in roughly 20 years. A blast from the past as they say. He was there with the wife and the in-laws. The same guy who thought all girls were dumb doll heads the last time I saw him. Had to wrap my head around that change. He tells me he's become a coach for the local football club. The pay isn't thrilling or anything but it's still better than punching in and out in some office job. I told him genuinely that I reckoned it was a great job. Very fulfilling. I genuinely meant it because, if I'm being truthful, I wish I had thought of it for myself. Then it occurred to me. In all the years I spent in school being told that I needed a backup plan, that being a footballer is a one in a million-chance thing, that I need to focus and do better, so I don't end up with no job prospects. How come no one told me I didn't have to throw the baby with the bathwater? That's a ghastly expression but you know what I'm getting at right?*

/

Sitting in the music room. Gab's mum is sitting next to her on the piano stool, both backs turned to the piano. Her dad standing her mother side, hunched, looking over his wife's shoulder at the document she's holding. Gab looks at us and says: *It's my school report. My mum is about to read the conclusion out loud.* Mum reads: *We commend Gabrielle's drive and continuous efforts in music and literature. However, we must remind her that a well-rounded education is crucial. Therefore it is important that Gabrielle starts to put more work into the other subjects and not solely the ones she already enjoys as we feel she might benefit from cultivating new interests and skills.* Gab silently counts down from 3 with her fingers. Her mother adds *Geez, it's not like you're failing in the other subjects. Babe is it me or does this sound like a dig at us?* Gab: *Mum always feels like other teachers look down on her and dad for being 'lowly' music teachers. To be fair to her, some definitely do. My dad is kind of oblivious to all that.* Gab's dad: *I don't babe, I think you might be reading a little too much into it. They're just saying that she's bright and could do better in the other subjects.* Gab: *we better leave them, they're about to argue and that usually leads to them asking me to go get bread or something. They're always done by the time I get back. Mum, Dad, I'm going to Mo's.* She walks out of the room. Soon out of the apartment complex. She is walking down the street. Toward us.

They're great honestly. My dad is super mellow. Although that could be because he smokes weed with his coffee in the morning. I think he's just not a worrier. As long as he's got us and his guitars he's good. My mum is another story. She is beating herself up from not being a prodigy and not pushing one out of her vagina. Boob milk with a side of piano was my diet. First to train my ear and then my fingers. But it did nothing. I'm not even better than her. But I do have a better ear and voice. And she's

very excited about it. My dad just loves that he's got a pal to jam with. They got divorced late—cause my dad's perpetual cloud of weed and they're make up sex did nothing to chill my mum out I guess. She walks into another building. Climbs the stairs to the ground floor apartments and walks into number 24. Through the hall to the third door on the right. To find her and her dad sitting on a brown leather sofa watching tv. *I was 16 going on 17, my dad and I were watching reruns of the old Addams Family series, when he said: that! That is kind of like your mother. The* **'that'** *in question is Morticia cutting the head of the roses. 'Ugh?' I went. 'She kinda cuts the head off of everything good in her life.' Moment of silence because let's face it I'm a 16 yd and this is very deep and uncomfortable. 'Word!'* Narrator Gab facepalms herself. *Look at her. Anyway, despite the cautionary tale, I graduated and became a waitress to support my 'career'. Career which consists of uploading videos of myself playing the piano and singing, or just singing, on youtube and waiting to be discovered. Fame or failure. Nothing in between in my mind. And without fame, everything was just headless flowers. And like my mum, but unlike Morticia, I didn't see the beauty in it. I became pebble-eyed.*
Ash, walking alongside Mo, takes Gab's free hand in his.

On the way back from the train tracks, Nora is walking alongside her parents. Her mind is narrators-free. She's just aware of the soft grass under her scandals
of the fizzy cacophony of community
of the nettle-like drone of bugs around her
of jasmine tea warmth of the sun
of the sweet & cool mint bond that sometimes feel like puppet strings, sometimes feel like the string of a kite.
of the compass beating against her chest.
It's not that there's nothing under her mushroom cap, it's just that she's neither looking from the outside in nor the inside out. She's merely looking, hearing, smelling, feeling. *Merely.*

We zoom out and
walk eastward.
East of where we've left our chronology.

The One with All the Scenes inside of Phoebs's Pillow

INT: HOUSE - KITCHEN - EARLY MORNING

Gab & Window & Kar

A zesty Gab. Twisting one half of an orange. Pressing it down. Releasing all the juice. Pouring the juice from the juicer into one of the 8 tall glasses. Twisting the other half of the orange down against the heads of the juicer.

♩I had a hard time waking this morning

I got a lotta things on my mind

Like those friends of yours

They keep bringing me down

Just hangin 'round all the time ♩

Gab looks up. Out the window. Sees Kar's legs outside. Gab stretches up. Standing on her tiptoes to get a good view of Kar. By herself. Sitting on a bean bag and looking at the sky. Looking out to the garden. Toward the orange trees.

3 glasses full. 5 to go. The filled glasses are all adorned with a single orange slice balancing on its rim.

While her body proceeds with the task, her mind is on the other side of the glass.

Morning's bird breath & coffee's clucking & glass's cellophane silence

Ellipsis

OUT - TRAIN TRACKS - EARLY AFTERNOON

Everyone & Hyphens & Bridges

Verbena scented light.

The Coms and the Foreign Four stand by a big, draped thing on the tracks. About two metres tall & four metres long.

Everyone's visor-handed against the sun's sting.

Abe & Ash stand out. Facing the crowd not the draped object.

"I'm so glad we decided to unveil this today." Abe's pithy statement.

Ash pulls on the tarp. Gently at first. Then giving a few robust tugs.

A railcar. The bare bones of a railcar at least. Made of wood & wrought iron.

From the outside they can see the bare-boned insides through a rectangular glass-less window almost the length of the railcar. Ash gives it a push to showcase the iron wheels' ability to spin. Tamed. It doesn't chug, it barks.

"Kudos to Ash, who helped me finish it. Somehow it all lines up perfectly."

Groups take turns inside.

"It's only a symbol. Like a hyphen. But it's meant to be a bridge."

A bridge out of their paradigm island.

Motionless equivalencies. What he means is: it's a slow train coming.

The perplex hmms of one-track minds & plumes of barks & the acoustic requiem of a rosemary portion

INT HOUSE - LIVING-ROOM - LATE MORNING

An Elephant & Chiaroscuro & An Exit & Veiled lovers

Emma sits on the sofa. By the elephant side table. On it, a tea whistles an anise air.

Her birthmark is showing. She's wearing a jumpsuit with cut-out shoulders.

There's a blackberry fragrance about her despite the vanilla light. She's not yolk-eyed anymore. If anything, in this light, she's amber-eyed.

She's put her wants & needs on the shortest straw and picked it. She'll be back.

She's waiting for Ash to walk back into the room with the aforementioned present.

She looks out the window. Out to the garden. Out to the orange groves. The same avid way she'd watch a tv.

The vanilla light gilds her complexion.

Ash walks in and places himself right in front her. Now she's only lit from behind.

His birthmark is showing. He's wearing a green crew-neck t-shirt, jean shorts and no bandana.

He carries something wrapped in black and gold damask fabric.

He crouches down as she takes the object and removes the fabric.

He looks up at her & her amber eyes & gilded features.

A candle lantern. Copper bed & wooden chamber. Beautiful wood carvings.

Mingling light & darkness.

They kiss. *MWAH*!

"I wrote you something. It's upstairs."

"I'll get it." He straightens up, "Where is it?"

"Drawer. Bedside table."

He kisses her again. *MWAH* and heads for the door.

Bubbly trumpeting & the rubbing fabric of veiled *MWAHS* & adamant door swings.

EXT: GRASS BY THE BUS - LATE AFTERNOON

Soluble overheads & Cocking Cocktails & Colourful minimalist mindset & A gggeneration

Overhead compartments loaded with whims & '*wills.*' All suitcases adjacent.

They're in a cumulus. Nebulous & iridescent. Around them, beer blond light.

They're playing UNO. The most popular game in the Community. A matching game in which less is more.

BAM! Now it's plus 16!

Loudly points out Nora, exhilarated.

Ash's ears redden as he picks up the 16 cards.

Colour?

Green

Nora, 3 cards in hand, gets to dictate the terms.

Gab is humming

♪ If your memory serves you well

We were going to meet again and wait ♪

So, Nor', what do Abe & Ela make of you leaving again?

Kar inquires. Adding a green 0 to the pile of played cards. 3 cards.

They're ok. Different baggage, different journey.

Mo's arrows set the turns spinning counterclockwise. 8 cards in hand.

You and I got the same baggage and were raised together and we're still pretty different.

Kar's stuck. She draws from the Draw Pile.

Ash puts down a green and a red +2. *Pay back.* He's down to 19 cards. Nora smiles at him. He smiles back. His eyes meet Mo's & Gab's. They know.

Cause we don't actually have the same baggage.

Nora sets down a wild card. *Yellow.*

Gab sets down 3 9s. One yellow. One green. One red. 10 cards in hand.

The overhead compartment suddenly thickens. Pastis white.

Sometimes it seems like you're rejecting it because it was handed to you.

Hab puts a +4 down. *Uno. Sorry baby. Blue.*

Rob adds 4 cards to his 5. And puts down a blue 6

You could be right. I dunno. What I do know is my instinct tells me I need to go so I'm going.

Gotta do what feels right. Gab absent-mindedly adds, looking at the suddenly overcast sky.

Emma puts down 4 3s of each colour. Yellow at the top. Down to 2 cards.

Mo puts down two skips. Green at the top. 6 cards.

Sure, if you can afford it. Emma chimes in.

All eyes on her.

The pastis white ramps up. Rounding. Greying. Yet, somehow, the beer blond light remains intact.

Nora puts down 3 arrows. Red on top. Clockwise. Counterclockwise and back to clockwise.

Alright, Ash. Let's see what you've got. Teasing.

I got options. Thanks to you. Slams 4 2s. Yellow on top

Kar drops a wild card. *Green.*

Mo. 1 green. *Gotta admit I kinda miss my job.*

Several: *No?*

Emma draws from the Draw Pile. +4. *So sorry Rob. You're not having much luck. Yellow.*

Rob smiles. Appreciating her concern. *I'm fine, Em'. You're so sweet.* Puts down 2 skips. Red on top. *Muahahah.*

Nora *uno!* 2 6s down. Blue on top.

I do. I'm not doing too bad. The customers are pretty chill. I get time to do my own thing. Pay's fine.

What about all the others who get left by the wayside because of the system? Kar.

Ash. Blue 8.

I dunno. Maybe it's selfish, but I genuinely don't think I can fix everything for everyone else. I don't mind carpooling once in a while, but I mostly mind my own business.

That is selfish. Puts 2 blue 0s. *I win.*

Sweetie, and don't take this the wrong please, but isn't it what your folks did?

Kar stares, pebble-eyed, at Gab. Until raindrops beckon her gaze up.

They spring to their feet.

Shit. Where to?

The water dissolves their overhead compartments.

The house?

Yeah / to the house / Hurry / Fuck, it's lashing

They run down to the house

missing the tequila spiked rainbow. Thick. Frothy. Yellow & orange. Yet with a seemingly hard outer edge, like a rind. On the rim of the Community. Inside and outside.

Unresolved ideological horns bantering & The fizz of a dissolving marching band & rubbing n pitter-pattering of reshuffling

INT: THE O'S HOUSE - LIVING-ROOM - LATE NIGHT

Mo & Hab n Rob & Nora & Sugar

On the paisley clad sofa or the damask rug. Sipping mojitos by the honey light of the floor lamp. It sweetens the colours of the room:

From rust to tangerine

From Basque red to cherry

From hickory to cinnamon

From turmeric to canary

COOL CLINKS

Sugar, sugar billows from the turntable like steam from a hot chocolate.

Nora—sitting on the damask rug—away with on a white rum & lime & mint carpet ride, twists her pansy hair. The twisting sprouts orange thought bubbles. Which peels to reveal 4 people. Backlit. The four that had folded into 2 and that folded into 1.

Nora.

What is it with her and groups of 4 people?

She doesn't need her cardinal points to locate herself anymore. They're just her friends now. Especially Mo. The kitchen crack is gone.

SLUUUUUURP SYPHONS THE PAISLEY AND DAMASK PATTERNS

CLINK THEY'RE BACK

Mo—sitting on the paisley sofa—seeing through the spinning ice & white rum black n white spiral goggles. Still better than through glass. Eyes on Nora. A new light on her that he has the full picture. Of himself. Like Clark donning the cape & the form-fitting costume. Eyes on Rob. Eyes on Hab. Eyes on both as they *MWAH*. The kitchen crack is gone. So are the glass shards. Well not entirely. They're pending.

He's got something to explore now. Something to make out of this. Callas?

All 4 slur a storyboard of projects for the next few weeks.

Hab & Rob are ready to fill their eyes to the brim.

Nora is not quite done with another set of cardinal points.

Mo can't wait to reach the nearest phone booth and see the world with Superman's vision.

The Archies gummy hearts & onomatopoeia hiccups & the gurgle of a pending hibiscus fresh sunrise

Something Like an Encore or a Credit Cookie: Putting the Genie Back in the Party

EXT: WIDE SHOT - STREET OUTSIDE A HOUSE - FISHEYE LENS - SUNRISE

Somewhere, a rotary phone *zuuuuum* & *clicks* back to its initial position.

Static or constellation sight (depending on if you're glass half full or half mottled kinda person)

Traffic is like a clogged toilet. Except honking doesn't flush shit & cursing is just splashing yourself with your own fecal cordial.

Out getting the dough or being the dough. Money's still the yeast.

Rare are those flatbread days.

A magpie flies away with a ripped bag of crisps.

Maimed pigeons nod their way forward.

A lonesome bus stop with a frying-bench & a map that pins you to your spot.

Phones ring & vibrate. All the same somehow high & low hanging fruit.

Hipsters with airpods & air max-shod feet while grievances are to be aired out in the streets later that day and choked out with tear-gas & the mermaid wags her long consumerist finger from their paper cup.

INT: HOUSE - MULTIPLE CLOSEUPS - SHOULDER SHAKINESS - FROZEN GLASS FILTER - DIM LIT

Not anachronistically, the party's still here. Albeit anarchistically decomposing. The catastroph-ish remnants of cough-syrup-catheter free catharsis. All had the Molotov in them. All they required to have a blast was a cocktail. All decomposing. Along lines. Along acid rain lines. Along party lines.

KITCHEN

Condom wrapper n shoe still in the sink. Pending attention. Like notifications. Kiwi-
ish green fur & jellified brown barf & dust & plates & mails (e or regular) & *We
didn't start this* fired! & overdraft charges.

The biscuit poster *phewwwwwws!*

Floor caked with crumbs & ashes & hair & hairs & all of it is dust-crusted. Dust. The
equaliser. No trickle down. No hoarding.

Cig butts butthead with torn beer labels. Unsent messages in green, brown, see-
through bottles.

Up, surmounting the kitchen cabinets, elephants are gagged by absence.

A few towels too & vowels from scraped uvula & a slurred vomit nova.

Respectively under the sink and in the back kitchen, the rubber gloves & the hoover
are itching to get to work.

On the formica table, toilet paper, in their smallest square unit, made more
authoritative by Roman numerals, make, all together, a staggering, bumbling
'MANIFESTO', subtitled 'life hacks'.

LIVING-ROOM / SITTING-ROOM

The sofa barf has mated with the one on the right armrest & a handball size ball of
tissues held together by spent joy cum-eagerness & turns out the Silent Majority was
the condom, and the Revolution has cum in it

Conservative condom. Ironic. Or, maybe, the Revolution was just a big jerk off.

Knives taped to the Voltaire chair for an HBO homage.

Sticky rings on all the surfaces. Ringing revolutions muffled by revolving doors &
doormat treatments or doormat mentality.

Somewhat discreetly, this narrator sits astride the harp and plucks its strings as if it
could erode the bone-riddled bedrock. Erode something that comes a-riding the
slogan of your favourite cereals. Passing for vitamins when it's really Viagra.

TOILET or LOO or JOHNS

A drooling toilet bowl & *Anthony was here* bottom right corner of the door cornered
with this wedgie-strophic mess cornered with wedgie wages wedged between the
black toes of the wealthy

BEDROOMS

4 rooms & a den

Drool & dream-filled pillows.

Collective insanity remains in the communal space, where it belongs.

These are individual pockets of sanity-ish-ness.

– One with a skatepark vibe of urban accommodations & street revelations. Doodles & disses & dope shout outs deface the ivy illustrations of the wallpaper. A dartboard clock. Both darts on 4. A THRASHER sticker on a Magic 8-ball. Stray zippers for a pending project. A Lego Death Star. Bookshelves dedicated to DVDs & video games. A receipt pick with cinema ticket stubs and topped with a knob for safety reasons. A hookah –

– One like a watercolour painting. Not meek or subdued. Simply unmoored to the page. Seemingly floating.

Unlike the pins on the map that adorns the wall perpendicular to the dressing-table. There's also a collage portrait over the head of the bed: multicoloured pansy spirals as hair, Nora features drawn with pencil. Tie & dye watercolour skin. Gothic rose – windows for eyes & lotus mouth. Clad in star anise. A paper mosaic moon hovering over her –

– One with clothes (clean n worn), coins, bills, a harmonica, a phone charger, a Donkey Kong loaded Gameboy, a bottle of Nina Ricci perfume, bracelets, music sheets all helter-skelter—despite many a shelter—on the floor. A synth with seemingly doorless keys—only for the lobby-minded—and a flaxen and massive chest of drawers serving as a platform for a framed exhibit—possible name: Things or People & Me. Sparrows & nightingales inhabit the wallpaper –

– The last one, combed to perfection. Done preening, just displaying. Taking after the peacock in vanity, curves, & colour palette. A hamsa nailed to the wall by the door. A chalkboard mood ring ringing in the latest algorithmic mishmash of creativity. Dug out of the gram & the old neuron search engine.

Callas in a heart-shaped clay vase. In through the artery. Pencil drawn ads for the store. Some lithe & floral with long-haired women (the latter captive in the intersecting rings of representations of another gram—a venn one) carrying paint trays with paint flower blobs. Poppy red. Daffodil yellow. Pink hollyhock. Calla Lilywhite. Zinnia green. Brunnera blue. All meant to be technicolourised with watercolours.

Pending on the trestle—the only thing that's grams and gramps passed down
mahogany furniture—screen printings. Confectionery. Gummy bear dyes-

The tightly and highly strung horse neighs but can't deny. Some things can be blue
pills and still genuinely make you hard.

GARDEN

Barf besmirched beanbags. Feral and flailing. Overrun with pompously puffy
dandelions, plantains, white clovers, and wild violets. Ants & birds have feasted on
the crumbs & the barf too. Someone, or something, has dug in the flattish belly of the
earth. Purpose unknown. Possibly instinct?

THANK YOUS

So grateful to *Dead Skunk Mag, The Literary Canteen* and *Querencia Press* who respectively published 'Whistle While You Work', 'Excavating the Homesick's Blues' & 'A Brain Freeze, Coppers & Squares' and introduced *Acid Taste: Excavating the Homesick's Blues* to the world.

Thank you to Emily Perkovich (and Querencia) for not only being the wind in my sails but fostering a collaboration that even this teamwork-adverse writer could enjoy.

To the benevolent teachers and professors who got me here. I was always somewhat remote, even in my favourite subjects, despite a sometimes-annoying eagerness, but when my life was especially challenging you made learning a safe space.
To my found families across the Channel.

To my friends who listen to my rambling rants and nonsensical whims

To my amazingly supportive partner

I'm so unbelievably lucky to have you all.

To the grandfather who's always with me.

And a final, not uncomplicated thank you to the family that raised me and shaped me. You did your best.

ACKNOWLEDGEMENTS (AND A POTENTIAL PLAYLIST):

1. The title was inspired by The Merry Pranksters' notorious 'acid test' as well as the wild book Tom Wolfe wrote about it. Not to mention one of my favourite Bob Dylan songs: *Subterranean Homesick Blues.*

2. 'Something Like a Throwback or a Look Back: Pulpy Ride & Rocked Out Oranges & Can You Dig It?' refers to The Who's *Magic Bus*, Fleetwood Mac's album *Rumours* and The Mammas and Pappas' song *California Dreamin'.*

3. 'Nondescript Day' uses lyrics from The Fugs' *Carpe Diem.*

4. 'Practical Pranking' uses lyrics from *Les Cactus* by Jacques Dutronc.

5. 'Whistle While You Work' is a nod to Disney's famously industrious dwarfs (*Snow White*).

6. 'Earshot' uses lyrics from Joni Mitchell's *California.*

7. 'Deflated Paper Buoy' uses lyrics from *On a Night Like This* by Bob Dylan

8. 'Invisible Ink on Popping Petals' refers to a work by Alfons Mucha 'Biscuits Lefevre Utile'

9. 'Whirly Pop' uses lyrics from Jefferson Airplane's *Somebody to Love*, Serge Gainsbourg's *The Initials B.B,* and The Grateful Dead's *One More Saturday Night.*

10. 'Peach Grooving' uses lyrics from *Stuck in the Middle With You* by The Stealers Wheel.

11. 'Super Realistic Slice of Time' uses lyrics from *Electric Ladyland* by The Jimi Hendrix Experience.

12. The 'Tripping on the Dark Geography of Light's Empire' refers to Magritte's work *L'Empire des lumières* and uses lyrics from the folk song *500 Miles* by Hedy West.

13. 'Acoustic Brewing' alludes to Lewis Carroll's famous smoking caterpillar.

14. 'Embroidered Denim-Tracks in the Prairies' uses the title lyrics of The Byrds *Turn!Turn!Turn!*

15. 'A Rainbow of Loading Irises & Cough Syrup Phoniness & Clipped Musings & Itchy-Sideburns Reality' alludes to J.K. Rowling's Voldemort as well as his horcruxes and uses lyrics from Manu Chao's *Me gustas tù*.

16. 'Tugging at the Wooden Neck Sticking Out of the Rear-view Mirror of the Lemon Licked Charabanc' uses lyrics from A-ha's *Take On Me* and The Fugs' *Carpe Diem*.

17. 'Outta Sight' to the French band Téléphone and their song *Un autre monde*.

18. 'A Handless Bullseye But Mostly an Eliciting, & Perhaps Illicit, Tea Time' refers to Jean de La Fontaine adaption of Aesop's *The Hare and The Tortoise*. It also refers to *Time Has Come Today* by The Chambers Brothers.

19. 'Framed, Colour Laden & Popping' uses lyrics from *Comic Strip* by Serge Gainsbourg. It also refers to characters from the following series or films: *I Love Lucy, West Side Story, Titanic, Friends, How I Met Your Mother, Malcom & Marie*. There is also a nod to Robert Indian's dizzy *Love*.

20. 'Those Desert Sights' refers to Bob Dylan's *One Too Many Morning*.

21. 'Bouquets or Sprigs of Radio Solstice' refers to Donovan's *Sunshine Superman* and René Magritte's painting: *Ceci n'est pas une pipe*.

22. 'A Morphing Ballad of Figuration (part 2)Kitchen Sink Magic & A Lack of Vitamin C Flare Up n Deference' uses the following songs: *Livin' on a Prayer* (Bon Jovi), *A Minha Casinha* (Xutos & Pontapes), *Tainted Love* (Depeche Mode), *L'aventurier* (Indochine), *Take On Me* (A-ha), *Marcia Baila* (Rita Mitsouko), *A Town Called Malice* (The Jam), *Let's Dance* (David Bowie), *Fiesta en América* (Chayanne), *Like a Praye*r (Madonna), *The Times They Are A-Changin'* & *My Back Pages* (Bob Dylan) and *The Circle Game* (Joni Mitchell).

23. 'Prior: Lifting the Mushroom Cap to Find Baked In & Rambling Narrators & Narratives' alludes or directly refers to *How I Met Your Mother, Ally McBeal, The Big Lebowski, The Catcher in the Rye, Ferris Bueller's Day Off, Veronica Mars, Fleabag*.

24. The title 'The One with All the Scenes inside of Phoebs's Pillow' alludes to *Friends*. It also refers to *Orange Juice Blues* by Richard Manuel, *Generation* by The Who, *This Wheel's on Fire* by Bob Dylan and Rick Danko, and *Sugar Sugar* by The Archies

25. 'Something Like an Encore or a Credit Cookie: Putting the Genie Back in the Party' alludes to Billy Joel's *We Didn't Start This Fire*.